T0207891

Letting Go of Eltanzer

LETTING GO OF
ELTANZER

ROBERT L. WOOLEY

LETTING GO OF ELTANZER

This is a work of fiction. All of the characters, names, incidents, organizations, and dialogue in this novel are either the products of the author's imagination or are used fictitiously.

iUniverse books may be ordered through booksellers or by contacting:

iUniverse
1663 Liberty Drive
Bloomington, IN 47403
www.iuniverse.com
1-800-Authors (1-800-288-4677)

Because of the dynamic nature of the Internet, any web addresses or links contained in this book may have changed since publication and may no longer be valid. The views expressed in this work are solely those of the author and do not necessarily reflect the views of the publisher, and the publisher hereby disclaims any responsibility for them.

Any people depicted in stock imagery provided by Thinkstock are models, and such images are being used for illustrative purposes only. Certain stock imagery © Thinkstock.

ISBN: 978-1-5320-0032-4 (sc)
ISBN: 978-1-5320-0033-1 (e)

Library of Congress Control Number: 2016910071

Print information available on the last page.

iUniverse rev. date: 07/06/2016

Man cannot live on fantasy alone

Eltanzer

When I was very young I came to know something strange. I was sitting by a clump of blood root, seeming at one with the radiance of snow white blossoms perched on blood red stems. It was a moment of unity with something very powerful. I was alive and in love with this place, the place I called home.

As time went on, other things of fanatical wonder entered my existence. For example, one day the mystery of dogwood flowers erupted into my world. I saw a stunning array of fantastic colors and patterns against a clear blue sky. Then a scholarly 2nd grade girl informed me this was the tree that her lord was crucified upon. The girl explained the crossed blossoms of cream petals had rusty nail marks at their tips and a crown of thorns. I did not know at the time just what that all meant. She did not know either. It was something she learned from wise grown-ups. She was taught this is a temporal place on a journey to another existence known as heaven. This notion of there being another place above and beyond was a very strange thing to me. It was the first time I came to know there was a split between the world I was in and another. I could not reconcile the existence of the blood root with any other realm. Thinking about a world I could not see or feel made me wonder what was real. Was it this place or another? A lot of wise men assured me of the truth of unseen places. It sometimes made me wonder if I was defective, even nuts, as some call those who don't get it. Often I would just ignore what wise men taught and go into the woods and immerse myself in the glory of great murmuring trees. They seemed to speak a language I understood. As time went on I actually became divergent. I did not fit in so well with society. *Id est* with the clans of people in old eastern American towns. There were norms young hominids were required to obey, occupations to aspire to, and eastern society to fit into. Talking to murmuring trees was not among them. In middle school I even pulled my school desk out of its row into an isle all by itself. The teacher called me Philip Nolan, the man without a country. I suppose that was just a little below the guy he called Charlie the Loud Mouth. Pulling a desk out of a class I did not fit into so well was just *res ipsa loquiter* in my opinion. My teachers did not understand stuff like that in those days. That is really all I am going to say about my 1950's formal education. Except, I will review a few truths I was supposed to believe in at one time or another that I could never observe as happening. In my world, bodies did not overcome gravity and rise into the sky. People did not survive in fired furnaces; dead people did not rise out of graves. For a short period I was supposed to believe storks delivered babies, and Santa Claus delivered Christmas toys via a deer drawn flying sled. I could fill the rest of this book with this stuff. But I will be merciful and not do so.

As I grew older I discovered I did have a strange place in my mind where I could imagine things. I started to see where some of the things I did not formerly believe in might have come from. I found for example I could even create imaginary people if I needed to. I could make a tree talk or even a lawn mower. I found only in my mind could I find numbers. I thus became a formalist as regards mathematics. I was not a Platonist who believed numbers could be discovered in nature by looking for them. The only thing I was sure of is that my mind existed and it could contemplate weird mental constructs like numbers. I could also choose things. Sometimes I chose to believe, as the ancient Greek story tellers seemed to believe, in flying horses and gods who controlled the fates. I could even go outside at night and find the flying horse in the sky. Constellations these star patterns were called. But I had to use my imagination to see the horse or the maiden in chains, or her mother that looked a lot more like a crummy W to me. The scorpion looked the most real to me. I saw it in the southern sky of summer above my lake, the lake I grew up by and on and often in. The lake was in a glacier gouged bowl in the Eastern Geological Highland Province. Someone told me scorpions lived in the western deserts, places very different from the verdant forests of my home. There were stories about the sky people and things like scorpions. Because of my imagination I could appreciate the story telling. I did not think anyone named Orion was bitten by the scorpion and actually died and was placed in the winter sky as was claimed in the Greek myth. But they were interesting stories that seemed at least metaphors of reality. Sometimes my mind lived in a world shrouded in a dense fog. Sometimes it saw shining mountains rising high above the fog. The mountains I kept seeing were shown to me in a very small black and white snapshot taken by a young woman who went on a trip and climbed them. She climbed The Grand Tetons in a far away place called the West. She said it was very different there, not like this place at all. I wondered if that place was imaginary or a different real world? In my mind I created from the small snapshot a towering mountain range. I more or less grew my own mountains with my imagination. The place called the West became a mysterious place with mystical giant shining mountains. I wondered if I was crazy for making these glowing lofty crags seem real in my mind. I had heard people were deemed crazy if they made up imaginary worlds and then lived in them.

Of course, as I got older, I had days when I wondered if I was not crazy at all. Rather maybe all the people around me were nuts. I seemed to know some things that no one else did. I knew there were large chestnut logs on the bottom of my lake. This one old grouch said you are nuts. Logs on the bottom of lakes rot. You are seeing things. But I had dived, holding my breath, and I saw the logs and touched them. I had evidence. In addition there seemed so many who didn't know a thing about what scientists discovered in the last four hundred or so years. A lot has been learned in just my lifetime. Are those who don't know about these scientific findings and believe in stories, thousands of years old, of creation by gods, nuts? Or am I nuts for believing stories that have been developed in modern times that are in conflict with those ancient beliefs? The seminal thinkers seem very rare to me and the people who understand what they have to say about reality are slow to catch on. It often takes twenty to thirty years for even the intelligentsia to gain widespread knowledge of a new seminal discovery. Let me tell you one seminal discovery that just bashes my mind. Bacteria arose almost four billion years ago. They are all over the place but we can't see them they are so small. They are like one micron wide to three microns long. Not only have they been around some four billion years there are huge numbers of them in every human body. There are some ten of them for every animal cell that makes us up. They most likely are what created us. Over eons they created us.

Having grasped the idea that one's mind could sometimes be at cross-purposes with itself about what it believed, I discovered there was another raging fire in my consciousness. It was not until much later in my life after I had moved my home from the East to the West. That came about, I suppose, by a restless spirit inside me that wanted to explore places I had never been. It was quite a few years later and a big mess was created in my mind. It was as if I was madly in love with two gorgeous women. Two at the same time and this, as most of us know, is a hopeless quagmire. It is just not legal or ethical. It is, I suppose, legal if you are a firm polygamist like in some countries but in my culture it is not legal. That is very strange too. Because my country is mostly Judeo Christian in it's religious beliefs. And the founding fathers of the Judeo part were all polygamists. Abraham had at lest two wives. Jacob had two, Leah and Rachel. And Rachel gave him another to boot. But today we have decided that one man should have just one wife. We also added this odd thing called "marriage." And we said just one wife per man. It is not very practical to have more than one wife per man either if you ask me. If one lady wants red curtains and the other blue curtains, it is just a mess. There are other messes that get made but I won't go into them right now. It just opens up too many cans of worms. It is my kind of luck that both women would hate worms and scream and carry on if worms got out of the can. So I had to do something. I had to clean up and mend this festering sore. I had to decide if I was going to live in the East or the West. I had chosen a place called the West to make my home and I was in love with the place. But something from my past kept vying for my attention. If I did not mend the sore I felt some nebulous substance would just ooze out of the wound and splatter on the ground. Then it would seep into the ground and disappear. I really did not know if I could resolve the whole mess but I just had to give it a try.

I should say here that the festering mental abscess arose because I felt I had lost something. Something that was very important to me. Something I was in love with. It was very hard to think about it. It hurt whenever I thought about it. I fell in love again but I could never forget my first love. Maybe it is what losing your childhood sweetheart to an accidental death is like. So I did not think about it as much as I could, or should have. I worked hard on not thinking about it. It was painful and very disruptive when I did think about it. Sometimes, when I dwelled on it too much it made me very crazy. I don't remember exactly when it was. Somewhere in time I knew I must find what I believed and make a home in what I conceived as reality.

I would remember things. I could not stop remembering things. I would sometimes be all by myself in a sea of sagebrush on the Snake River plain. There the pungent perfume of that arid land dweller filled the air and seduced me into intense love with her sage green beauty. If a pronghorn happened to stop by and notice me I often became enrapt. I was definitely in love with this land. Then without warning I would remember places and being part of places that in a different, a younger life, I was as much in love with as I was with the sage lands. I would recall sitting on a large granite boulder that had been moved from someplace in the North to where I was sitting on it. It was moved by the Wisconsin ice sheet. While sitting on the boulder I was contemplating the scaly plates of a shagbark hickory tree and wondering how that scruffy bark happened to be. Most trees did not have this kind of exfoliating bark. Hickory was different. Like me. I was most in love with that hickory tree. It was very strong too. I remembered things like taking my little kayak onto my lake and leaning back just letting it bob on the gentle waves making a gurgle sound under its bow. There were water-lily patches all along the lakeshore that put forth amazing scented water nymphs that changed with the seasons. Some were snow white lilies some pink. Others had yellow blooms that looked more like yellow ping pong balls when they were closed. There were bass and pickerel that hid under the lily pads that could be challenged with bass bugs and Heddon river runts. The hills were gentle in slope and could be climbed without a great deal of exertion. Except on hot August days. Then the humidity and heat would cause the heart to work hard. During August nights katydids sang in the tree tops and crickets from the ground. Fireflies came in the mid summer and spangled the night with love flashes. In the fall acorns littered the ground from giant oaks. Squirrels of several kinds collected these for winter fare. The seasons were very distinct with autumn shouting in screaming colors, while winter seemed to just put the ground and life to sleep under a white snow blanket. In the spring that started in February the landscape stirred and sap ran in the maple trees. Soon spring peepers adorned the evening with frog music. It all took hold in my mind, the sights, the feel, the smell, and the sounds of a place that was once familiar, home.

I often longed to return to my first love, but in a split second my new love grasped my soul. It was as if she was a jealous woman who would not share any past loves. "You belong to me now!" the strong voice of the Great Basin once roared. And I am a jealous basin and now you know you love me and I must have all of you.

Now this started to tear me apart. I had chosen this new love of my own free will. Before my brain was fully grown I had gone to the American West and seen The Grand Tetons and the desert where the scorpion lives. I had, with young legs, climbed the fir shrouded Rocky Mountains and stared into the Grand Canyon. I fell for the grandeur just as if it was a stunning woman of irresistible charm who drew me into her mysterious domain like it or not. I stayed and began a career as a forester in the west. Yet I could not forget my former love, had eruptive periods where I wanted to be only in love with her, the quiet but utterly stunning beauty of the East. It was a dilemma. Sometimes it drove me nuts. As time went on I wondered if I was a foreigner in the place I lived or had I become so covered with western dust that I was now the same as native born. But I did not want to ever forget my first love either.

Now I must say many westerners considered easterners in abject contempt. "Ya either a man or a easterner," one of my crew bosses blared into my eardrum on this barbed wire fencing crew I worked on. It was a good thing I am a peace loving animal or there might have been blood as I am no short shrift at a hard left to the jaw if need be. I remembered my boyhood hero, easterner Theodore Roosevelt, came upon this crap and more or less won grudging respect through toughness at the right time. So I worked hard to suppress my rage.

This stuff about where I belonged, where home was, why I could not stop loving the eastern white pine and the western sugar pine but not be in the arms of both just got to working on my spirit. I just had to mend it.

I found someone, or perhaps I should say some fantasy more like Tinkerbelle, to go over things with. I named her Starlight and she was very bright. Now when I say Starlight, I mean Starlight. I don't want anyone to be confused about this. I am not trying to be upscale or metaphorical about it, or condescending either. I just want to be very clear about Starlight. Starlight came from the night sky on clear nights, swirled into my messed up brain and became gorgeous and very understanding.

Starlight began one night by asking, "What is one of the first things you remember?"

"I remember a time before my country was broken. There were small towns and rural apple orchards that made cider in the autumn. Sometimes the cider got left in a crock and something happened. I distinctly remember watching Mother of Vinegar hard at work. There was not a lot to look at and I got bored. Eventually I got so bored I tasted the amber fluid. I mean what else could you do? That is when I crashed into a revelation. The world has taste as well as a visual identity. This was all very mysterious as far as I was concerned. Did you know it was an organism that was doing all the work I could not see?"

"An organism?" She asked with upturned eyebrows that did not much make me feel comfortable. I was more or less, mostly less, comfortable. It was a real fig Newton.

"Yes, it was an organism the biologists call *Acetobacter aceti.* The biologists renamed Mother of Vinegar to *Acetobacter aceti.*

"Does it make you uncomfortable that the biologists did this?"

"Yes, well, I mean not exactly, actually no is what I am trying to accomplish here."

"Just when did you taste the vinegar?"

"It must have been when I was three years three months five days and 17 hours old. I just don't think it occurred before that."

"So very young. Is there anything significant about that?"

"First I need to establish a firm fig Newton. Nuts, I mean premise or two."

"You said 'fig Newton' first. That doesn't make sense. Then you said premise. I am confused. Oh well, never mind, go on."

"The first premise is that humans emerge out of biology. Did you know this was not known for most of human history? In fact, in terms of geologic time and even in the flash of human existence, it is just amazing how recent it was that humans figured this out. It was, for instance, thought in most of history by most people that a human came from a seed planted by a man into an incubator called a woman who was similar to a bed of soil into which plant seeds were sown. There likely was a small handful who we believe were seminal thinkers who knew otherwise but they have been kept in the shadows of history. It was simply too dangerous to let them into the light. Their ideas were anathema to those in power, to those who benefited by an ignorant swarm of servants. This finding that a woman was a co-creator of the baby she carried was at odds with revelation. Science was overturning revelation and this was dangerous.

"What does this have to do with your problem?"

"I emerged out of biology. I am biological. It is biological things that have emotions, and feeling and get all messed up in their tangled up biological nerve circuits. If I was a piece of mica schist I would not care one wit about memories. I would not have any! But I emerged out of biology, and I have ancestors whose lives and genes and way of making a living are still in me."

"Yes, there is a long history and it is not written down until just very recently."

"Even recently, where they did write things down, we are not sure how many thought otherwise because they often did not write conflicting ideas with their culture. They did not write as it would have been damning evidence of heresy or rebellion against the big *Homo* Kahuna, or papa *Gorilla* or the clan of the *Pan,* the chief of the tribe or the emperor of the state... At a minimum they would have been smacked or bitten, ostracized, ridiculed, condemned as insane. Some were locked in dungeons, others burned at the stake, impaled, or crucified. All for just coming forth with new ideas. This biological ignorance lasted rather close in time span to the amount of time it took to re-discover the idea of the Greek thinker Aristarchus; that the earth moved around the sun or heliocentric model of the solar system as opposed to the geocentric hubris that reined in the dark ages."

"You have an interesting conglomeration of animals and people in there."

"Is there really a distinction?"

"Let's assume not for now. Your mind seems to be running on high octane. It is all over the map. You cannot keep a single coherent thought before you tangle with another. Some of it is just babbling," Starlight whispered.

"Also there really weren't any Dark Ages either. There is not a shred of evidence the sun did not spew forth photons, plants absorbed photons and, in many parts of the world, human minds illuminated ignorance with inventions and insights. It was just in some parts of the northern hemisphere that anathema of natural reality reigned and thus got referred to later as the Dark Ages."

"Please go on."

"Then one of the greatest seminal discoverers of all time named Antonie van Leeuwenhoek made these vastly improved microscopes that could magnify 275 or more times. And he saw what we now call bacteria. And blood cells, and single celled animacules, and spermatozoa. He had to collect his own spermatozoa during intercourse with a woman so as not to incur the wrath of his church and culture by the other common means of emitting semen. Emitting spermatozoa in other ways without proper absolution and penance could subject one's very soul to eternal damnation. Antonie was smart enough to avoid that trap. Now Mr. van Leeuwenhoek made his discoveries in 1677. It did not of course prove anything. The spermatozoa could have been a complete human or homunculus as they called it in those days. Now hardly anyone knows his name. Even worse those who do know his name don't know how to pronounce it properly. Does that sound unjust to you?"

"Yes, I suppose so."

"Right. Of course another epidemic of injustice broke out. It was not for another 150 years until Carl Ernst Von Baer discovered that female mammals produce eggs. It was widely known that chickens and other birds lay eggs and these hatch into baby birds of a feather, but now it was demonstrated that women who were still considered chattel property by and large, incapable of intellectual achievement by and large, incapable of participation in the governance of free democratic republics by either serving in legislative, judicial or executive branches or even capable of casting a sensible vote for testosterone sacks with whiskers who did warm chairs in governing councils. At least that was a theory of what they did when they were not playing cards, smoking cigars, surrounding bottled spirits, or settling matters of honor with instruments of dueling or war cannons, swords, or muskets. No it took until 1827 to see the female produced something that appeared to contribute more than just a warm bed of soil for the next generation to incubate in. Injustice; for the female was not given one ounce of credit for being involved in the design of the newborn."

"That still does not answer the question of participation by the female as far as design or creation does it?"

"No, that has to wait until Mendelian genetics is digested, and then again until 1953 when Watson and Crick show a plausible model for the genetic code that gets sorted out by the process of cells reducing the chromosome number from diploid in somatic cells to haploid in reproductive cells such as spermatozoa and egg."

"Can I..."

"I would like to introject at this junction how mad I am, I mean I am enraged and very angry that Gannett Peak in the Wind River Range of Western Wyoming is the highest point in the State of Wyoming at 13, 804 feet above sea level while Grand Teton is not the highest point in Wyoming at 13, 770 feet above sea level."

"That seems a strange thing to be so irate over."

"It is not so strange to me, madam. Darn it, just like a flash flood had hit me I entered a fantasy of walking in an acorn storm. The kind that happened in the oak forests I grew up in. They happened after the first frosts of autumn brought the acorns out of the trees and made great scatters on the ground. It was the time of year when school had just started and these pretty young girls walked in their brand new school dresses with pert legs skidding on the strewn acorns and I was immediately in love with it all. I have these kinds of sudden realities from time to time. They can make me feel so lost some times. Lost in a vast unknown. You know don't you, your Excellency, Miss Starlight?

"Maybe you get into a funk about Mountains to slap down your intense feeling of loss. Could that be what this mountain rage is all about?"

"What? What did you say?"

"I am just trying to understand something." Starlight replied.

"I would now read a poem. It is the only thing that gets me over things like those fools who found the disparity between those mountains and could not keep it a secret. I mean how could Grand Teton not be the highest peak in Wyoming? Gad it pisses me off."

"Please, you need not get so worked up about this with me anymore. I get it."

"I am sorry I do have to get worked up about this. It is too important to just let go. That is one of the things I find enscoriating. If no one ever gets enscoriated things like this just keep getting perpetuated. Next thing you know two thousand years goes by and these things are set in granite."

"Enscoriating? Is that a word? Oh never mind. Please, let's try reading the poem."

"Ok, if you fig Newton. I mean exist. I mean if you insist. I wish you would stop making me so nervous."

> Time and barrels of wine
>   Seem sublime things to me.
> The Valleys of the Napa,
>   The Willamette, and Wenatchee
> Are more enrapting because of it
>   To me.
>
> The rivers flow, the water sparkles,
>   The wine ages, time passes.
> I watch the river flow and see the wine
>   sparkle when the time has passed as it
> rightly must. Then as it is written *In*
>   *Vino Veritas*, I find the spirit in the wine
> And join the river as it flows through time.
>   Time and rivers and barrels of wine
> Seem sublime things to me.

"Thank you. Now that wasn't so hard was it? I like the poem. Are you the poet?"

"I don't think so. Maybe. I don't know."

We have been going a long time today. I think that is enough for today."

"You like the poem? There must be something the matter with you. Most would say it is not a poem at all. No sir, I mean mam, not a poem at all. Hard for me to deal with I will tell you that right now too. Hard to deal with."

"We will take it up again. At our next encounter."

The night was awful. I tossed and turned and snorted and caught my sleeve on one of the bed stands and knocked the telephone off its base and the alarm clock. Also a glass of water with ice cubes in it that splattered all over the floor and even got the sheet wet where it splashed like a bull moose had masturbated on it. The telephone started howling and making a beeping sound. I no sooner got this all put back together and was ready to try sleep again when there was a flash of light then the distant roar of thunder. That got me pretty well aroused I can say. Thunder storms always get me more aroused than nights that are calm and hot or winter nights that are calm and cold, or even spring nights that are neither too hot nor too cold. Sometimes in the spring night, though, you could smell the new life coming out of the ground or hear peeping sounds, or creaking croaking kind of sounds when new life comes alive from some odd hibernation in the cold ground or from thawing ponds. Thunder did it tonight. Sure did. Awoke some sleeping neurons and made them think about how frogs could emerge. Got me thinking about where they came from, how frogs happen to be. No one in his right mind would design frogs to be the way they are. Only a crazy goof off, that's for sure. It was on those warm spring nights that the frog choruses livened the dark. And in this lake I lived by, bass splashed along the shore. They came to the shore to feed on bugs that fell from overhanging birch trees. And frogs that ventured off the shallow muds into dangerous waters.

I was not real anxious to encounter Starlight today. Not at all, especially if discussion of the poem came up. I do not like discussion of poems such as that one that showed up on a piece of scrap paper one time not too long ago and I was caught with a pencil in my writing hand. The paper was not designed for use as writing either, it was wrapping paper, dark brown kind, the kind we used to tie string around and put in the mail. And there it was and I got caught as the probable writer. It really pissed me off I will tell you. That was not supposed to ever see the light of day. I don't think I was even supposed to see it. Now I was going to have to talk about it. Well, I made up my mind not to talk about it. I would deflect the conversation to something else, I decided. I will make a pre-emptive strike, I said as I entered the door. In my opinion that is the only way to ever handle discussion of a poem. Poems are undiscussable. Period!

"Good morning. What is this list you have put on my tableu solan?"

Thomas Paine
Common Sense
The Age of Reason

Thomas Jefferson
Declaration of Independence

Governor Morris
U.S. Constitution

Benjamin Franklin
The Autobiography

The Journals of Lewis and Clark Meriwether Lewis and William Clark
Nathaniel Hawthorne
The Scarlet Letter

Henry David Thoreau
Walden

William Cullen Bryant
Thanatopsis

Alexis deToqueville
Democracy in America

Edgar Allen Poe
The Raven

James Fennimore Cooper
The Last of the Mohegans

Harriet Beecher Stowe
Uncle Tom's Cabin

Dred Scot decision USSC

Abraham Lincoln
The Gettysburg Address

Mark Twain
Tom Sawyer
Huckleberry Finn
Roughing It
The Innocents Abroad

Theodore Dreiser
Sister Carrie

Edith Wharton
House of Mirth

F. Scott Fitzgerald
The Great Gatsby

John Steinbeck
The Grapes of Wrath

Robert L. Wooley

East of Eden
Of Mice and Men

Upton Sinclair
The Jungle

Sinclair Lewis
Main Street
Babbitt
It Can't Happen Here
Elmer Gantry

Ernest Hemingway
The Sun also Rises
For Whom the Bell Tolls

Jack Kerouac
On the Road

J.D Salinger
The Catcher in the Rye

Harper Lee
To Kill a Mockingbird

Aldo Leopold
A Sand County Almanac

Edward Abbey
Desert Solitaire
Black Sun
The Journey Home
Abbey's Road

Carl Sagan
Cosmos
Shadows of Forgotten Ancestors

Lynn Margulis
Microcosmos

Stephen J. Gould
Wonderful Life
The Mismeasure of Man

James Gleick
Genius

Robert Pirsig
Zen and the Art of Motorcycle Maintenance

Wallace Stegner
All the Little Live Things

"Easy. It is my minimalist list of literary works that one wishing to have a remote chance of knowing anything about America would not only have perused but read over and again until they see the entire corpus, the zeitgeist of the country."

"Zeitgeist?"

"The spirit of their times."

"What do the books show?"

"Simple, that despite the overall, generally accepted view of my fellow citizens that humans, especially Americans, are rational they are not rational, especially Americans. The books and writings as a corpus show just how hard it has been to form a society of humans who rose above the two million or more years of our natural biological decent in dominance submission clans, tribes, and even larger cohorts known as kingdoms or nations. Moreover they show nothing of a particularly intelligent, rational, sane, or brilliant mass of hominids that make up the self proclaimed most advanced nation that has ever existed on this earth."

"Can you please explain that to me?"

"Just a minute; it makes me so darn Beethoven mad that Grand Teton is the high point of what the aboriginals of the area called Teewinot that means Many Peaks. And there it is when you look at the Cathedral group the highest sharpest peak sticking into the sky. Teewinot is right next to her but lower and of course some insignificant third sharp pointed peak that I can't remember the name of. O wait a minute I think it is coming. It makes me so bilious mad that we have named every single stinking ridge, peak, with some one's name that often has nothing to do with the mountain range in the first place. It is Johnson peak that is the other of the three. I think. I am not very confident that that is the name of the other one. I wish no one had named any of the peaks. Except of course Grand Teton. It seems a great thing to name a range such as the Grand Tetons after what some French trappers, probably horny as the day is long, and by the way I am convinced, saw from the west side where they do look like what the French said they look like; *Le trios tetons*. They should have left it at that. I don't mind calling them Le Grand Tetons or the Grand Teton Range or Teewinot, what the aboriginals called them 'many peaks.'"

"That's enough. Stop."

"I named a mountain myself once. The thing was huge. I got lost on it too. Could not find my way home. Eventually I found my way out and looked at it from a distance. At that moment I called it by its proper name, I think, I am not sure. 'Holy schist.' That was it Holy Schist Mountain. I suppose Mount Santa Feces is what the cartographers will enter if it does not already have a name and I tell them where and which one. Of course they would not be allowed to call it what I called it. Of course not! The United States Geological Survey would censor that. Naturally they would. But I think I won't report it to the cartographers. It would just cause too much trouble. I think I will just keep it a private matter between me and the mountain."

"This naming of mountains is surely a big issue for you. But I think it is a cover up. I think you are covering up something that hurts you and won't let the festering sore see the light of day and fresh air and get healed. What do you have to say about that?"

"I don't know. I think it is the impermanence of things. Names of mountains come and go. Like Teewinot. Then along comes some human name. Nobody today ever heard of the human name. I don't like things to change that much. I don't like wasting my time remembering all these mountain names, especially the ones that have nothing to do with the mountain. Grand Teton does so fine, great in fact. It just flows from nature that it should be the grand one of the many peaks. I might be ok with a few named for people who did noble things. Pike's peak is fine since Pike never desecrated it by climbing it. He did not build a road to the top either. He just watched it from a distance. But we were talking about books anyway. The books show the United States of America, my native land, is becoming unstable. Not that it ever was stable mind you. The British should have won the American Revolution hands down but they didn't."

"Why?"

"The British existed under a monarchy with strong cultural reverberations of our natural heritage in dominance submission hierarchies."

"You have not finished the first thought about the books before the next diatribe about the Grand Tetons that just doesn't seem to connect with the list of books. Then before you answer my question about the anger from naming mountains we are off on the British. Can we resolve just one issue before going on to anything else?"

"Sure, there was a woman approached me yesterday. Well, that is not entirely correct; actually I approached her when I went to sit on the seat in the back of the bus we were both riding in to a business location along the Columbia River. I could tell you more about the business but it would take too long so I will just tell you about the woman. Actually she was more or less a young woman, much younger than I would say I am. Any way she said she was a feminist! Can you believe it; she just blasts that out at me after we have been riding in the back of this bus for some time. I was trying to sort out feminist, communist, socialist, socialite when she flat out assaults me with what I clearly recognize as baloney. She says, I look old enough to be one of the screwed up men who were raised by a bunch of suppressed wimpy women ruled over by their husbands with an iron hand, the kind that should be abolished from the earth and by god they will be by the kind of woman she is. I thought it best to ask her if she was a geologist at this point. I was really interested in whether she was a geologist because there were some interesting geological features passing by our bus windows and I was interested in the opinion of a geologist about them."

"Was she a geologist?"

"I just remembered the name of the other peak in the Cathedral Group of the Grand Tetons. It is Mt Owen. I don't know where I conjured up Mt Johnson instead of Owen. Of course that is what it is. I don't know why the boobs had to go and mess up Teewinot with a name like that. I mean that is truly droll. Exceptionally boring. I don't know why little facts like naming all the mountain peaks has to clutter up our maps, our landscape, and our minds. But there is hardly a pimple on the landscape that doesn't bear the name of someone no one ever heard of. As if it is of supreme importance that their name on the mountain means they did something sublime and everyone gasps and bows their head in honor of the great one whose name is on a map of the mountain. And furthermore, it still galls the hell out of me that Grand Teton is not the highest point in the whole State of Wyoming."

"Even though you explained it quite well before. This anger seems to keep cropping up. Like it is just stuck there."

"I am not going to name any mountains right now. You are going to use some kind of trick on me. Probably some Freudian psychological trick. That is all bunk you know. I mean about Freud, except for the stuff he got right. The stuff he got wrong he got really wrong you know, but the stuff he got right, he got really right. And no one in my native land knows the stuff he got right just the stuff he got wrong. In fact you can't even talk about it all it is so screwed up out there."

"Very well, but I think we should try to remove the anger since it is not helping you."

"Now I was telling you about the feminist and her arrogant super superiority complex. The she –knows- it- all, nose- in- the- air, big deal me, kind of first impression she made on me was not favorable. She would not even answer the question of whether she was a geologist. This infuriated me off good but I thought I saw a way to put her in her place. That would be like embarrassed, on the floor, red faced kind of, pusillanimous humiliation. So I just firmly informed her that the mothers who raised me were farm girls at a time when being farm girls meant they worked their asses off doing chores, excuse me, their pretty alluring darling little behinds off. Also helped milk cows, slop hogs, stack hay, paint barns, hoe weeds gather eggs, cut firewood, as well as learn to cook, pick and can peaches, and freeze sometimes on winter nights when the stove went out. These girls used a chamber pot and carried it out in the morning to the outhouse that I tell ya, was, in the winter, an icebox and stunk a lot. In the summer they were boiling hot and stunk a lot. Still they had great poetic character about them and they were not stingy about sharing it. There were no hot showers or bath tubs they could fill with just a turn of a faucet, and not much in the way of make-up, fancy leg shaving razors, shampoos and conditioners. Ya wanted a hot breakfast ya had to light a wood burning stove or if they were lucky an oil burning stove. Then to make matters worse along came the great depression that was fostered upon them by ignoramuses that controlled the money supply, and who screwed up the way credit works, the way commodity exchanges work, the way stocks and bonds work and ended up putting millions out of work in the cities and many family farms on the auction block. You would think these women would give up and just enter the prostitution profession or become Annie Oakley types or seers or that sort of thing. No! When the big war comes along they go to work in the factories making the weapons of the American military, the arms, the ammunitions, the boots, and growing the food on the farms that allowed the Western powers to defeat Imperial Japan and in concert with the incredible efforts and blood of the Russian people to prevail over the Nazi scourge. Then I said after all that, after working much of their lives in the beginning instead of having a career or profession in mid life and beyond, they chose to be mothers. Yes mothers, not stay- at- home- mothers or home makers, but mothers. They were damn good at it too I informed miss stuck up feminist snot. It might even be one of the things that is wrong with us now. In those days mothers were damn proud of their sons. They let us be boys too. Like we went out into the unfenced neighborhoods and climbed large trees and made forts in the woods, and caught frogs in the swamps, and turtles in the fields, and big black snakes. We made forts in the sumac and roamed the old decrepit apple orchards that were full of ghosts. We got bruises on our knees and poison ivy all over our bodies and burrs in our hair, and stung by bees. Our mothers always knew what to do. The place was safe too. The mothers formed bands who looked out for every one's kids at the same time. They kept the neighborhoods safe. I don't know if I made a single wimpy divot of an impression on the obnoxious creep on the bus. And frankly, I don't care. I just told her the truth and that was the best I could do. What do you think of that?"

"It sounds like you have a good deal of respect for your mothers."

I had to stop thinking about my mothers or I would sink into a remembering hole that I might get stuck in for a week. I fought with the hole like it was a spooky horse, got a grip on the saddle horn, and steadied the wide eyed steed. I said to myself ask something to get away from this critter.

"Have you ever seen the Grand Teton Range from the west side? Not many have seen them from the west as you have to go out of your way to get a good view. Even those who pass along the main North South Highway through the extinct Market Lake area of the Snake River basalt plains covered with big sagebrush usually at high interstate speeds don't see their very tops. It is not unusual for clouds or fog to occlude the view. To really see them you have to make a pretty good detour through potato growing farms and sagebrush that most people just don't care about. They go to McDonalds and stuff French fries down their gullets but they don't want to know where they come from. I find that all execrable."

Suddenly I crawled through a worm hole into my past. I was sitting over the oval of a two-hole outhouse with a tin roof. Mulberries from a giant overhanging Mulberry tree were plinking on the tin. The place had an olfactory sensation of mulberry scented excrement that I was trying hard to add to with limited success, so I just had to sit there contemplating the aroma in the dimly lit half moon waiting for nature to do what had to be done to get out into the open air again. I worried about taking too much time and that some additional clients might show up and become impatient. Eventually I added a nice addition to the composting sludge, some white fiber, pulled up my shorts first, jeans next, and was quite elated. I opened the door, was dazzled by the sunlight, and found no other irate folks in line. It was a grand moment. As suddenly as I went into it, I pulled out of this waking dream of a few minutes of attention to nature's duty when I was still very young. Darn these flashbacks, they blast into my life and just take over for a minute and I feel a great loss of a simple time I once loved that is no more. Drat. Fell off the critter again.

I heard Starlight speak.

"Let's discuss your fascination with the Grand Teton Range."

"Ok, presidential campaigns are interesting. Here is the way I see it. We elect our President every four years in accordance with the part of our constitution dealing with the executive branch. We all know the president is very powerful being delegated the commander in chief rank of the American military among other duties. The president is over all the administrative departments including the Department of the Interior that includes the U.S. National Park Service that oversees Grand Teton National Park wherein currently the Grand Teton Range rises as its main feature. I doubt if the range gives a pickled poop whether it is in a national park but I am more favorable than unfavorable about this. It is more a matter that no selfish money grubber can fence it so that I can never see the range or get up close to the heart of the place, feel the granite rocks or touch the alpine firs and spruces that swath their lower slopes. That reminds me, I have to write another letter to the editor to get the Alpine Fir named the Alpine Fir again. It used to be the Alpine Fir but some nit picking technocrat said wait a minute Alpine means above tree line. You can't name a tree Abovetreeline tree. So from now on we will call it Subalpine Fir *Abies lasicarpa*. Now this stinks. This really made me mad. Look, Alpine Fir is a beautiful poetic name for a tree. Subalpine fir is burdensome, cumbered with technocrats, un-poetic, boring, and stupid. I thought about this. A lot I thought about it. I am a forester you know. Then one day I ascended this mountain through dense stands of Alpine firs. They were so magnificent; they were standing at attention reaching for the heavens, like they were good friends of god. I kept going higher and higher and the trees became shorter and shorter until they were nothing but mats close to the ground. That is when it hit me. A tree is a woody plant that is at least twelve feet high. Clearly these were not twelve feet high but botanically they were the same species as the sentinels lower down. Both were *Abies lasiocarpa*. So these alpine dwellers were just suppressed by the strong winds and deep snows of the alpine tundra. Ergo the species was correctly named in the first place Alpine fir. Isn't that grand like one of Robert Frost poems? Alpine firs are a poem of the Grand Teton range and all the other mountains they adorn in the west. I was so happy when I cleared this matter in my mind."

The Alpine Fir

Spire of the night.
Guardian of Mountain heights
  Unafraid of starlit nights.
Strong alpine winds cannot this fir
  Affright.
A tree of soft but sturdy might.

For mountain goers a gorgeous sight.
In twilight fir gives forth, soft rum like light.
  And stands strong against cold wintry bites
Of wind howling on mountain heights
  In close acquaintance with starlight
Immersed in the mystery of starlit night.

Sage of immense and quiet might.
  In awesome beauty fir prevails
And stands its ground in life's travails.

"I am glad you got that cleared in your mind. It does seem like a good solution to me even though I would not know an Alpine Fir from any other tree."

"That is one of the things that is wrong with us. Don't you see it? It is no wonder we have so much trouble electing presidents. Nobody knows what they are doing. Most don't have a clue what the man in the job does anyway. Do you realize the most important thing done by the president is not usually done by the president?"

"No. but I suspect you can explain it to me?"

"Look ever since Yorktown when Admiral DeGrasse shows up with the French Fleet the winner of national disputes has been the one with the best navy. That was proved again when the British navy dropped off a fair number of troops on the mainland of the new American nation, drove its president, that would be Madison, who a lot of girls are now named but not boys, from the dinner table over to a battery of canons and burned the white house down. It was, I admit, a close call when the Imperial Japanese Navy transported some troops to some American territories and held some American ground until our navy took it back."

"What does that have to do with the most important thing the president does?"

"How can you not see it?" The big deal, the really big deal, is the president must keep the U.S. Navy second to none. We are located on the earth such that no foreign powers can reach us easily and the navy fills in the gaps. Keeping those sea lanes open to free commerce is a big deal for our economy. The president, of course, doesn't do any of the actual operation of ships. Certainly we would not condone such a travesty as having the president swab decks. Or operate engines. Or shoot missiles."

"Well no I suppose not."

"Anyway back to what I was saying. After running the navy the most important thing the president does is keep places like the Grand Tetons a place where every single citizen, whether a little bit crazy, crazy, or insane, can get well. They can keep the holy Alpine Fir free from the wrath of Satan. To do this the president must first recognize that he or she is the leader of a nation that is not united, never has been united, and never will be united. We were fractured in the beginning and remain so. Look at the few presidents most Americans regard as great. The ones on Mt Rushmore come to mind. They all led a disunited, quarreling, bunch of tribes. The tribes even included idiots in their dues paying members. The trick was to know the union was quite a bit more imperfect than Gouvenor Morris implied when he wrote the first purpose in the preamble of the U.S. Constitution was to form a more perfect union. It was a pretty crappy union at that time. So the successful presidents find some small thing they can do such as preserve the Grand Canyon from money grubbers that the obstinate tribes might at least respect. Of course even the great ones will never get all the people. To this day we have the Washington haters, the Lincoln haters, and both TR and FDR have a following of detractors."

"Interesting hypothesis."

"I was walking along the Wind River, to the south of The Grand Tetons, on the other side of Togwatee Pass. It was late fall. Not many people were there. Pretty much alone I would say. That is when I came to the trees."

"Came to what trees?"

"I was very intently focused. It was like a deep meditative state where I was united with the cosmos or something. There were candy stripped hills to the east and red rocks of the Chugwater formation. I heard my lungs breathing, the air making a murmur in my windpipe. I heard my very own heart beating quietly in the wilderness. The serenity, the serenity, was as quiet as when two lovers kiss for the first time."

"Are you awake? Are you ok? Starlight asked"

"Oh, there you are, I thought you went away,"

"No, I thought you went away. Where were you?"

"I was with the Tacamahac. In my mind that is."

"The what?"

"The beautiful Tacamahac. *Populus tacamahaca.*"

"I don't understand."

"No, no one understands. It just pisses me off what they did to the Tacamahac, the most sublime hardwood tree of the Wind River Valley."

"What did they do to it?"

"Those swine renamed it the Balsam Poplar *Populus balsamifera.* I am telling you I am so mad about this if I run into those creeps out there along the Wind River I cannot be responsible for what happens. Now don't get me wrong I love the Balsam Fir of the east and if any jerk messes with trying to rename it, well there is going to be a haggle. So it is not Balsam I am arguing about, no it is changing the haunting name Tacamahac to Balsam that sets me into a rage. They have no right!"

"You do take these things hard. I was going to ask you sometime. What is a forester?"

"Here is what I think. I think most people, when the presidential campaigns are underway, look at three things. I think they look at the candidate's biography a little bit. Not so much as to really persuade them. I would for example take a second look at any candidates who were born in a log cabin in Kentucky. Not that that would be the deciding factor in my vote. But it would be a factor. Next I think we find out something about the character of the candidate when they are out campaigning and making stump speeches, and doing interviews, and eating all that crap that causes heart attacks and diabetes, and being heckled by idiots, bigots, and stinkpots. I always look to see what makes them get red in the face, or say something really dumb, or lose their cool, or scratch their crotch when they think no one is looking. But here is the thing most people miss. I look to see if they have presidential knowledge."

"Presidential knowledge?"

"Yeah, isn't that cool?"

"How do you know if they have presidential knowledge?"

"Yeah, that's a good one. No one can tell if they have presidential knowledge. No sir, no one. There is no test ever invented to show if they have presidential knowledge. Isn't that amazing. Before we let doctors practice medicine they have to take a lot of tests and pass them. Before we let lawyers practice we make them pass the bar exam. You can't even get a high school diploma without passing a test. But presidential candidates…. we don't even require them to pass a test that shows they know what continent China is on, or what the blast radius of a five megaton nuclear warhead is, or who owns the national debt of the United States. Now I could care less if the president doesn't know what an archiocyathid is. Simply because it is not necessary to the job of being president. But if a candidate did not know the difference between a Sunni Muslim and a Shiite Muslim, that president could involve us in an internecine tribal war that has been going on for centuries. This has happened in my short lifespan."

"So how does one determine if a candidate has presidential knowledge?"

"That is the mystery. We can't. We can only sort out the ones who demonstrate they don't have it.

"I think we should let that be it for today. I might be better able to figure out what it is that we need to work out with you if I have a good night's rest. Somehow we must clear the mess in your mind."

"That is fine. I need to prepare my speech on inequality that now so threatens to put us into complete instability and start a violent conflict again. I remember when it flared up in the mid point of my life. We elected a president who sounded and talked like a commoner, a one of us. But he was a firm believer in the dominance submission hierarchy. He believed there is an elite, perhaps not more than ten percent of the

American population, who should rule, who should control the wealth, who the remainder should serve with admiration. Worship and serve like the ones whose names destroy the majesty of the mountains. They called it by the euphemism of "supply side economics." Some who saw what it really was called it "trickle down economics." It was the beginning of the wholesale slaughter of the American dream that everyone should have an equal chance to do what he was good at and to have enough wealth to be happy. It was a reversion to our two million year long evolutionary history of living and struggling in dominance submission hierarchies."

"You really do intrigue me. Still you are exhausting. I need a mindfulness break. You are a challenge. Perhaps I could ask you to try some homework. Could you try to focus your mind on just one subject, one thought tonight and keep it on that thought? Could you try that?"

"Yes sounds like fun."

The next morning.

"How did you do on your homework assignment?"

"I did well, I did it real good."

"Did you focus on just one thought?"

"Oh, yes. I focused all night from twilight till sleep. Except of course when I drifted off into this little fantasy where I was having a little knee patting thing with an alluring young lady or an older girl or a woman. I don't know which to call her. In this dream she was wearing nothing but these very lacy panties and she had big sparkling goggle eyes and Grand Tetons. Next I gave her a little pinch on her behind, and she squealed, and I got very aroused. Drat! I wasn't going to tell you about that. She was a very good friend of mine. Once. Did I tell you that? Did I tell you I was very very in love with her once? It made me a little crazy sometimes. When it got really bad, I even went to bars and splashed the crazy with iced bourbon just like it was a raging house fire that firemen douse with water. Did I tell you that?'

"Well not quite as adamantly as just now. But I do understand."

"I am not convinced you understand. I don't know that anyone understands that preposterous stuff that just floats into the deepest thoughts of one such as me focusing on a single thought. Then this stuff intrudes. It caused deflection."

"Deflection? Is that a word?"

"It must be. I just said it and it makes sense doesn't it?

"Let's try and see if you can get back on the thought you were focused on?"

"Ok, all you had to do is say so. I will not think about feminine lingerie at all. Now here is what I focused on. I saw this silk sheer see-through gown in a department store window and decided to buy it for her. No, rats, I am sorry. I will now hereby return to the single thought. I thought of this plant that should be on the alpine tundra of the Grand Teton Range. It is called Alpine Collomia and its scientific name is *Collomia debilis*. It is utterly smashingly beautiful when it blooms. It is so beautiful that even alligators never eat it. I am very careful, very, very, careful never to pee on it. No matter how bad I have to pee I never pee on it. There are not a whole lot of things I am that careful about not peeing on. But this one I am religious about not peeing on."

"I did not know alligators lived on the tundra of the Grand Tetons."

"Of course they don't. Where did you get a crazy idea like that?"

"Please continue."

"So I am focused on this problem. In my mind I see the Alpine Collomia brilliantly adorning the tundra of the Grand Tetons and it just really gets to bothering me. I can't solve it. I actually started getting mad at you for giving me this homework to do."

"What, mad again? About what?"

"That I could not solve the focused problem."

"The problem?"

"Right, you see the Alpine Collomia grows on the tundra of the Salt River Range to the southwest of the Grand Tetons. It grows on ranges north into Montana; it grows in the Cascade ranges of the Northwest. It grows on ranges all around the Grand Tetons but no reports of it growing on the Teton tundra have been made. Now you can see what kept me so focused. Why I was so absorbed. There was here a problem I could not solve. It was a real caladraciopus."

"I beg your pardon? A what?"

"Are you afraid of dying?"

"Yes, are you?"

"No. I was born to return to the great stream of not being that is pure being right from the beginning. Dying does not exist for those of us that understand this. Enjoyment of the great mystery of time must take precedence over worrying about it coming to an end. It does come to an end and our bacterial cells and the fungi, and various members of the arthropods and nematodes see to it that our molecules are returned to the earth, the soil, and the elements of their structure made available for use in some next generation of life. Many worry about a *dies irae* that is just a façade for not sitting in the eternal moment and standing in awe of the great achievement of orogeny before us. Do you see it? How can you not see it?"

"See what?"

"The flathead sandstone. It is kind of yellowish orangey and blocks of it are laying 6000 feet high on Mt Moran and then where you can't see it is 24,000 feet below the Jackson Hole Valley. Those rocks were once the bottom of an ocean that the geologists say transgressed on the North American Craton some 570 million years ago during a long existence of time called the Cambrian period. Isn't that a neat sounding program. The Cambrian program. There were strange beings that lived on those ocean floors. The acting was superb. Trilobites were the main characters and they were every bit as skilled as Clark Gable and Vivian Leigh were in *Gone With the Wind*. They were species of actors with names like *Anopleura* and *Gossypluera* but no one knows them much anymore. Hardly anyone knows Clark Gable or Vivian Leigh either except a few old hoary crowned living fossils.

"That stage you see was once all on the level. But today part of it has dropped to 24,000 feet below the valley floor and can only be known because some drill holes found it down there. It is just one piece of evidence that nothing stays the same. The earth is not fixed, it is constantly changing. The actors are not fixed they are changing too. The trilobites for example became extinct during the Permian period. So the trilobites were employed for some 250 to 270 million years. Probably cleaning rocks and sand of goop and algae. Not a bad job if you were a trilobite. Then poof, gone just like the old South in *Gone with the Wind* and something new arises."

"How many visitors to Grand Teton know about this? How many see what you just told me, do you think?"

"Oh, not that many. I ask people all the time about these things. Some times on the trail to Taggart Lake that brings a lot of em. It is a short trail so brings lots of feet that can make a couple miles but nothing like say a summit climb."

"Have you ever climbed to the summit?"

"Oh hells bells no." I never waste a minute on such a worthless waste of conscious time any more. I have never been to the summit of any mountain and found it was better than looking at the summit from below. So I stopped going to summits. It is like trying to find god. You go higher and higher and then it gets colder and colder and fog sets in and the air is so thin you can't get enough oxygen to your brain. Then you realize the closer you get to heaven that it really is not up there. The closer you get to god the farther away she is. And your brain complains about the lack of air and I have even seen people puke on their boots."

"Wait, I must make a note of that."

"No sir, I mean no mam, I would rather spend an hour with a lodgepole pine on the lower slopes or if I must do a little trudge upwardly, find a whitebark pine and contemplate the great time period these and their kin have resided on the earth. There is fossil wood of coniferous trees from the Triassic period. You can see it at places like Petrified Forest National Park in the Chinle formation. It is strewn all over the west from geologic formation after formation. You can find fossil wood in the landscape of a great circle drawn around Grand Teton as its center.

"There are even places around the youthful Grand Tetons where the ground is very ancient. There are places around the west I go to when I want to go home. I can't actually in reality go home you know. It no longer exists. That drives me nuts on many occasions. When I think about it; it drives me even crazier. I get so lonesome about it. It was done deliberately by people too. I just can't seem to escape the craziness of it all."

"You say you can never go home again. Why?"

"I went to the American West while still a teen. I wanted to be a forester or as it turned out more like a John Muir, or a Theodore Roosevelt. I wanted to live in a larger more untamed place than what still existed of the great Eastern wild lands of our fore fathers. It seemed so simple at the time. I fell in love with the great western trees, and the sagebrush deserts. The Cascade volcanoes, and the pronghorn rockets, the pasque flowers and the prairie rattlesnakes. I adored the blue grama grass and the alkali sacaton. The west was a land of great contrasts, lush mountain valleys and harsh lava lands. There was a vastness to the sky. She was wild the west was, compared to the soft gentle east. I fell for her too just like I once slipped into enrapturement with the east. I was smitten. It is a crazy thing, I know."

"Are you married? Starlight asked.

"No."

"Ever consider it?"

"Not as to date."

"Why not? You seem very impassionate. The kind of passion a woman would love to have in her man. Isn't there a real woman in your life?"

"I have not formed the ineffable bond. Not the secular bond of marriage that is just the government. I mean the ineffable bond that Adam and Eve formed in the holy book. They were not married. Did you know that? No where does it say they where married. They were husband and wife. You see there just was not any government around to call them married and extend governmental privileges or require governmental responsibilities be exercised."

"But you established an ineffable bond with something called the west, did you not?"

"Yes and with the East too."

"But you can only have one. And there in lies your craziness. That we must resolve! Maybe you need a real woman not this fantasy in your mind."

(A month later)

"I have been most worried about you. You did not come to see me or let anyone know of your whereabouts." Starlight said in a concerned voice.

"Did you not know that I would be about the great one's business?" I forcefully replied.

"What does that mean? No one knew where you were."

"It was right after the great snow. The whiteness covered everything. I just needed to contemplate the rocks. Those gneisses and schists that are over two billion years old. I wanted to think on them while I could not see them directly. Sometimes when you can't see something directly something right before your face your mind gets clouded. Haven't you ever had that happen?"

"I don't think so." She said with uplifted eyebrows.

"So I am watching the great white shroud and thinking of beautiful things like the snow on the boughs of the spruce trees. The trees had their cones still on a lot of branches like in a Christmas card. Then it happened. It happened so suddenly it scared the thermal underwear right up around my throat. I thought I was going to be strangled. I fought it though. I pulled it off my neck, but it was cold in that air. I mean it was really cold."

"What happened?"

"It was a specter, like a whoosh, a taloned harpy or that sort of thing that the ancient ones spoke of. It made a red splatter on the white snow. It was whiter snow than I had ever seen. It was like the purest flesh of the great goddess, Ashera I think was her name. The talons held the struggling victim. I could see the terror in its eyes. Then sharp curved knives began to tear at its neck while the talons held it tight. The warrior was hungry. I could feel it he was so hungry. He was so hungry there was no mercy in his heart. A spurt of red shot from the sacrifice. Right from its jugular vein I would say. It left its mark of little red beads on the white flesh of the mountain. The cold white flesh of the mountain. I stared and stared. I was so focused I thought of nothing else but the ritual before me."

"What was it that you saw?"

"I pulled out a notepad and wrote it down. There will come a time many years in the future when they are worshipping in the temple of the blood eater when they will need a first hand eyewitness account. The great thing deftly plucked each feather one by one and set it beside the sacrificial dove. The sacrifice still twitched now and then as its organs were made bare. I wrote it all down exactly as it occurred, exactly as was demanded. I wanted no mistakes. If there were any mistakes I would myself be condemned. Of that I was sure. It was imparted to me."

"Who imparted it to you?"

"It must have been Charlorain. It would have been the great Charlorain. Certainly it would have been. Of course she has no form, no being as a sentient being, but her beauty is so unsurpassed it drives you crazy. At least it drove me crazy. I was crazy for a long time you know. As far back as many years ago I was very split in half. But after I joined with her and she did things that made me just utterly explode from the tension and make a hell of a mess all over the place. Only in deep sleep while camping in a high fir forest could I escape from the whole bilious affliction. Grand iron water I tell you. When I joined Charlorain, even though I was still a lot in love with another, I could sometimes put the trouble aside and be not crazy. Just for a while, mind you, not forever or anything like that."

"Who is Charlorain? Where exactly did you meet her?"

"I might tell you sometime. I am not ready to tell you now. You would not understand it yet."

"You promise? Is Charlorain your real woman?"

"I will tell you sometime. For now I will take a rest and tell about something very real. I have to talk about something real now. Is that ok?"

"If you must. But we must begin to look into what makes you crazy."

"I want to tell you about The Great Caldera. Can I tell you about the caldera?"

"I think you are going to tell me about it whether I want you to or not. So open fire."

The Great Caldera

"It is hard to see it is so big. It moved along a path from the Owyhee basalts all across the Snake River plain. It blew its top about 1.8 million years ago, then again about 1.2 million years ago. It erupted again about 639,000 years ago. Now it resides just north of the Grand Tetons. If you just sit at the right place you can see it. You can see it in your mind steaming, boiling, and throwing red hot rockets and ash and smoke into the highest places. If you watch the eruption, and have like I have, watched the great creative power of these magnificent caldrons you can see creation in progress."

"What is it you are saying here? I thought volcanic eruptions are generally destructive. They cause disruptions in villages and people even get killed in them."

"Well, I have looked at the aftermath of volcanoes such as the ones in the Great Cascade Range and I think they generate new species of plants that heal the barren slopes, the ash piles, and pumice heaps. Penstemons come to mind. I worked with Penstemons you know. Ones that learned to heal the volcanic eruptions. Go and look at Cardwell's Penstemon on the blast zone of Mt Saint Helens sometime. You will see what I mean. The beautiful Cardwell swathing what appears devastation with a healing balm, a new creation.

"Ah nuts. I just made a warm mess down the inside of my leg. That happens when I think about those great eruptions. It is like you are watching her majesty get aroused and then things change in new and extraordinary ways. It is the same sort of mystery that happens when a woman gets aroused. You can always tell when she is aroused because her eyes get big, and there is an alluring sparkle in them, and then they invite you to come into her domain, and then they demand you to come into her domain, and satisfy her. You cannot stop it; you do not have power over your own body. Your penis is now in control of your mind. Your mind can no longer think about things like the Fibonacci series that may be involved in the way these eruptions takes place. Then you erupt. There is a violent uncontrolled spasm of your organs. Then there is peace, eternal peace. And sometimes the woman creates a new life, someone who never existed before."

"That is most astounding." Starlight said, most intrigued.

"Inside the caldera there is still boiling hot water that comes to the surface. Sometimes it spouts in great geysers of world renown. Sometimes it gushes out of clefts in the rocks and stinks and burns your penis, drat, I mean your nostrils, when you inhale it. There are places like the big hot spring named Grand Prismatic that have immense colors all around it. The colors are algae and very ancient organisms they call archea. They all have pigments in them and all the colors of the rainbow. There is also another kind of cell, the eubacteria. And Protista. And Chromista. When you look closely at them you see your very remote ancestors as far as I am concerned. Some of these strange single celled beings that live in the hot springs of the caldera are related to ones that live in our intestines and more and more we are coming to see that if they are working right we are working right and if not then we are not either. In fact the distinction between the bacteria in our guts that most humans despise, is just like any other organ. Without a heart we die, without a liver we die. Without a gut flora we die. That is the way of it. Once a person knows that they get a different perspective on things. Shit is the smell of the life force, even a creative force. Those little beings no one can see without a microscope are the life that showed up first billions of years ago right after the molten earth cooled. And there they are in the huge caldera to the north of the Grand Tetons."

"Your mind seems to just run away with you. Is it this way always?"

"I was in love once. Did you know that? Then I left her and that made me crazy for a long time."

"Tell me about it."

"I was at least a little bit in love with a brown eyed girl who had auburn hair. She was kind of a socialite or that sort of thing. She was a bit cliquey as a matter of fact. I ran into her at a soda fountain where everyone went for a chocolate sundae. She was with a bunch of her friends. I was carrying a couple of chocolate malteds to my friends and tripped and spilled malteds all over her dress. It was a mess. I have never failed to admit that. I have always owned up to that faux pax. A real man would do that. I never saw so much fire and disdain as the contempt that shot from her eyes. I almost changed my mind about owning up to these social blunders. It was close I shall assure you. Things like that happened to me from time to time. Some were fairly regular in their occurrence and some were more sporadic. I don't think it was as big of deal as she made it out to be but she never forgave me. I heard a long time later that she graduated from a very expensive school that was very famous and became a psychologist. Then one day a client who was very very rich and whom she was charging vast sums of money to come and talk to her about his problems came in the office one day, raped her, and then strangled her to death. It was all very extremely sad. I suppose I learned something of the random injustice that is ordained in this universe. There is evidence such as this that the universe just does not care a great deal even about its most sophisticated believers in their own superiority and worth. I mean this girl was a snot and a stuck up creep but she did not deserve that kind of retribution. In my opinion she did not deserve it that is. I have nothing other than my lowly not all that well supported opinion to render unto you in this matter. Nothing scientific or rational as the believers in rationality or justice or righteousness would say. I am not sure the bacteria that live in the caldera are going to do much better in the long term. I mean the caldera last erupted 639,000 years ago then before that it erupted 1.2 million years ago, then before that 1.8 million years ago. So it may erupt again any day now and it will be interesting to see if the bacteria in the springs survive. I think the answer to that is yes, a few will be lifted into the stratosphere on particles of the outer crust of the caldera and eventually they will plop back on some other spot on the earth and continue as if nothing ever happened. They have no need of windpipes that can be strangled by crazed nuts during talk therapies. This is currently just my own theory of course. But they say I am probably nuts. I am not sure if I am nuts or not. I am working hard on trying to figure that out. I actually sometimes pretend that instead of apologizing for my faux pas I just had congress with the poor girl I spilled the chocolate malted on. Just so she might have become less snotty, fallen head over high heels for me, and her life would have been spared. Now isn't that a crazy thing? Pretty messianic of me I suppose some would say. All I know is there are not that many people that I meet who will even talk about the things we have been talking about. Most of them are more interested in talking about shopping at Wal-Mart or whether they can get free miles on the airline they are going to fly on to go see their sister or brother in Hawaii or Norway or Georgia. There are only a few who think about the origin of things or much care that they don't think about those things at all."

"I think people's origin is important. Tell me something you remember."

"The forest was old, battered, and beautiful. The plundering ax men had been voracious. But they were not perfect. There was a small grove of white pines that had gotten some reprieve. They stood very straight and very tall. Once there must have been thousands and thousands. But they were claimed by the king and taken. In the cold slop of February I ran the maple trees on the bottom lands, down below these few spared sentinels on the hill. How did the ax men miss them? Only her majesty knows. But I think they were there for me. Cause while I emptied the sugar sap the pines spoke poems in the wind. And I told them:

> Maple sappy is sweet like taffy,
> But maple sugar is even gooder.

I could talk to trees back then."

"Those were the murmuring trees you once mentioned?"

"Yes."

"You miss them don't you?"

"I like the Snake River. It reminds me of snakes. I like snakes too. I am not saying I don't jump five feet in the air when I first see one or step on one, that sort of thing. I do. It may be one of those programs I told you about buried deep in my brain. I think it was but I can't remember exactly when. Maybe some one told me to watch out for snakes that they were very dangerous. I am reminded of something. I don't know what for sure. I think it is the timber rattlesnake I am reminded of. It is the most beautiful of all the rattlesnakes.

"The Snake River begins near the Grand Tetons doesn't it?"

"It really starts in Yellowstone if truth be told. Then it goes into a large lake. Now days, courtesy of hominids, it emerges from a dam that holds Jackson Lake. There are huge gates that it starts out with a blast from. Humans built that dam. I don't know how I feel about it either. Some people don't like dams. They can sure mess up things. This one supposedly keeps water for irrigation stored. They use it to grow potatoes that are stored, run through computer controlled canons that cut them into the exact same size. These strips are then boiled in a kind of oil that the advertising agencies have convinced our young population to eat a lot of. They don't tell the young people these oils used over and over again are changed chemically into fats that our body's enzymes cannot digest right. The oils then make the bricks used to make plaque in the arteries of people. The process used to be thought as occurring late in life and usually ended in a heart attack when the coronary arteries got clogged. Sometimes it clogged other arteries such as the carotids and the brain got starved for oxygenated blood and the neurons died and the person was often partially or completely paralyzed, or blinded, or lost their memory. Those events were known as strokes and they were and are quite common. Now in males it is now known that clogging of other arteries causes erectile dysfunction. They advertise all the time about this on the television. There is just not enough blood flow to the penis to make it stand at attention when a female wants it too or when you need to masturbate. Now I don't want to blame potatoes and the Snake River dam for every case of clogged up arteries. There are a lot of other culprits out there that participate too. Grains and sugar are building blocks of plaque in the arteries and the brain as well. It is even worse if you combine the altered fats with a lot of sugar. The trouble with grain is it also gets converted to sugar fast after you eat it. So add sugar from soda to sugar from grain such as bread, and sugar from potato starch, and then from pie, and candy, and muffins, and jam and jelly, and beer, and you can see where we have a lot of people who, if they get inflamed in their arteries, make gunk. I think anyone who wants to could go watch the roaring output of the Jackson Dam and think about what would happen if the iron gates and pipes started to rust up. If the rust kept building up because the iron reacted with the oxygen to make ferric oxide there would eventually be a lot of pressure build up. The water would back up and the lake would get bigger and the pressure would have to be released somewhere. The water might divert to some other outlet. Then the dam would stop flowing water down the Snake River. The cottonwoods you see all along it would become dry and die. That is how I look at it. There is a similar system in our body as you can see right there in the Grand Tetons if you look for it and use a little imagination. It is not an exact correlation just a metaphor kind of thing. But I doubt very many who stay at Dornan's or the Jackson Lake Lodge or the Colter Bay Lodge think about it the way I just went over. There were no vast empires of French fried potatoes in the days I am trying to tell you about, you know."

I got to reminiscing with myself at this point. I remembered going to see the great fire in the caldera in 1988. The fires were utterly enormous in size. They burned in these dense lodgepole pine forests for weeks on end. Now I have no idea what stopped them. They should have just kept burning. They should have burned south to the Grand Tetons. Then they should have burned the Wind River Range, and another prong should have burned the Salt River Range. Fire should have forged northwesterly up the Madison River, across the great boundary into West Yellowstone, a tourist town that once had a railroad station where luxurious trains brought tourists to see Yellowstone, the first of our National Parks. The 1988 fires could not have burned the railroad depot because the trains no longer ran there. Even the tracks are no longer in evidence. It was like before the great fires opened up the dense coniferous forests so tourist could see the place better that the best way to get there was wiped out by some invisible hand. The fires should have just kept going up the highlands above the Madison River into the Madison Range, roaring across the valley into the Gravelly Range, zigzagging into the Gallatin Range. Some fire fronts should have advanced into the Absorka and Beartooth ranges. Those by the way are named the Beartooth Range because a glacier of immense size and power carved one block of granite that looks like a Bear tooth. I am sorry for digressing so about the Beartooth, but I just couldn't stop myself. My point here is I have no idea why fires stop when and where they do. Except of course one idea I learned while fighting a big one once. When there is a high forest that blocks the sun, the wind, and the drying of the soil the fires just stop at those formidable barriers. I have tried to tell that to people who believe if you log the high forests you will lessen the wild fires that we in our infinite stupidity seem to hate. The truth is you will always increase the intensity and destruction of a wildfire by taking the high forest down. The place will dry up, and burn with extreme intensity. Not a couple years after the high forest is logged. No, it will occur forty to one hundred years after. Kind of an underhanded trick of her majesty I would say. Our dense brained pols of today fall for the trick time after time. Without a high forest that is maybe selectively logged to keep the shade on the ground they burn and then it will take hundreds of years to grow a high forest back.

"That bothers you a great deal I can see. Is that right?"

"Yes but not so much as it used to anyway. I have seen it over and over. Even from my beginning I have seen it. I can tell you. I am as you know a believer in the Medea Hypothesis. That is the theory proposed by a paleontologist named Bill Ward that species of organisms contribute to their own extinction. That may be a primary rule of ecology or how nature works. It could account for the observations we have made of the millions of species in the fossil record that are extinct. They would have been fine if they would not have helped with their own extinction. Isn't that beautiful. By the way despite some silly notions found in fantasy stories that we are not species, that is humans are something other than a species, the raw undeniable facts of life are simple. We are a species, and it may just be that the tremendous surge in the human population of this planet and some of the dumb stuff we do is just the law of nature at work. We may be hard at work on exterminating ourselves."

"Does that worry you? You are worrying me."

"No, I do not worry about such things anymore. In fact I think I will just go this week to Signal Mountain and listen to the elk bugle. People who go hear the elk bugle without the slightest interest in shooting the orchestra and hanging massive antlers in their dining room don't worry about things like that. As far as I am concerned the Eubacteria and probably the Archea are the modal organisms on this rather chaotic planet and they don't seem to give a hoot or a shit slick about who is extant or extinct. They just create some new arrangements and likely will fill the innards of some future menagerie of organisms the like of which we can not even come close to conceiving. I mean do you think before the fact we could have conceived of things like *Camarasaurus grandis*, or *Stegosaurus stenops*, *Triceratops*, *Protoceratops*, *Euryops*, *Goniophilus*, or flying pterosaurs. How many species of these wonders the kids call dinosaurs were created by her majesty, lived for millions of years then left only fossils to record their existence. We hominids have only been around for maybe two hundred thousand years with puny three million or so years of experiments to get to where we are. I have no idea either as to how a pterosaur such as *Anhaunguerra* ever managed to do what it took to make additional *Anhaunguerra*. I am still puzzled by how porcupines get anything done in that regard either. It must be tough for ol papa porky don't you think? I mean all that abatis around the playpen? There are a lot of things that seem inexplicable to me. I have no idea for example how mountain hemlock trees that grow around the Pacific Northwest ever grow up. Their tops are always flopped over pointing down. I might ask of anyone involved in that design which seems pretty much a non intelligent way to do things. That by the way is another thing I have concluded is not well understood by the mass of men. Practically nothing is especially well designed in the domains of living organisms. There is mostly a bunch of jury rigging, trying to make do with spare parts. But then this is a tough subject. It was much easier when a smart old man with a white beard was responsible and everything would become clear at some unspecified time in the future. That is after one dies it would all be made clear just what the plan is. In fact this is how I see it. If I die, and there is a heaven, and there is a fellow who looks like the portrait Mr. Michelangelo painted of him, and he is not the cranky, jealous, curmudgeon that many priests, elders, preachers and other apostles have presented him as, then this is what I would hope to find.

"Those upon entering would be greeted of course by the receptionist, Mr. Saintpetersberg. There are, as I suppose one of your erudition knows, many written legends and accounts of Mr. Saintpetersberg standing watch at the calcium-magnesium-carbon-oxygenated- hydrogenated gates. I will leave out here descriptions of the stunning statuary, bougainvillea and wisteria vines, geraniums in urns, birdbaths and hummingbirds flitting about, fireflies, harp playing angels and singing cherubim, boa constrictors, tarantulas, bull frogs, dragon flies, Sexton Beetles, and slime molds that I presume occur in so noted a place as the Pearly Gates.

I would say,' Hello Mr. Saintpetersberg, I am a biologist and I would like to discuss with the boss here how he created life.'

"You don't mean Mr. Dicotyledon do ya?"

"No I want to see his or her majesty, which created life."

"That is who created life?"

"His name is Mr. Dicotyledon?"

"Of course. That is who you asked about. Now before I take you in to see him or her I better check out a few things. First if you are a biologist then Mr. or Mrs. Dicotyledon will probably want to know a few things about you. For example he and she will want to know if you ever visited the Sonora desert and appreciated his or her giant most cactus."

"You mean the Giant Sagauro *Carnegia gigantea?*"

"Yes, I am sure that is the one. He is really proud of that job. He made the chassis and she made the flowers. And any biologist who has not seen one and appreciated it will usually get sent back for twenty five years and required to pick up beer cans, bottles, newspaper, pornographic clips, toilette paper and other items found often along roads in the western deserts where they last longer than Mrs. Dicotyledon believes is proper. Then if you spend enough time doing that and somehow get yourself to the Sonoran desert and appreciated this piece of artwork, you may get to

45

spend some time with him. If you are lucky her majesty will join you as she knows some things that he don't that most biologists want to know.'

"Anyway, if I get past the druids and the flower picking police this is how I would hope things might go."

"Oh please come in, good to meet you. Did you get to see my Giant Sagauro cactus?"

"Yes sir, they are I must say one of the finest poems I have ever laid eyes on. The prickles and pickles on those babes are utterly stupendous."

"Oh, that is music to my heart. Come on in here. Pull up a chair. Would you like a scotch on the rocks? I like a good scotch on the rocks. I'll tell ya those Scots sure figured out how to make a good scotch."
"Well, sir I don't actually drink…. Oh I suppose since you say it is ok it must be ok."

"It is fine. Now I shant kid you mind ya. I know her majesty may get a little wonky about it. But she is out in the garden right now. She and that old friend of hers, ah what was her name?? Oh ah, 'Eve.' They are still trying to get a few things sorted out. If you would rather we could have glass of Pinot Noir."

"Yes, I had too much scotch one time and fell in an outhouse that someone left the lid up. I don't ever want that to happen again."

"I remember that. Tried to warn you but you had had too much scotch."

"I even threw up on the rose bushes. Could we get back about the creation of life? Mr. Petersenberger said you sometimes tell biologists how you did that. I mean in the beginning, when there was darkness, no sky, or firmaments to stand on. Most people don't care how it was done. Just biologists. Oh, and of course paleontologists. And of course geologists. And crazy people."

"Ah shit, you can check out a video from the library. Goes through the whole thing. I get asked that so much I just put it on a video so everybody can watch it and everybody sees the same thing. I used to go through it with everyone but then her majesty came in one time and said I was telling it a little different each time and then I did not give her the right credit about one particular thing and she was pissed I will tell you. I, for example, said when I first worked on the problem of life I just made things huff up and divide. It was so simple. Then her majesty said I should make two kinds of living things. I should make one a male and one a female. She said things would get too lonesome all by themselves and I should make each one desire the other ya know. Well I said to her that if I did that there was gonna be trouble. She argued with me. I'll tell ya she argued and finally I said, 'alright, dear, we will give it a try. I will make females and males and there will be an attraction between em and they will all find the right attraction and join like a magnet joins iron or fleas to a dog. Then everything will be just fine."

"So Mrs. Dicotyledon came up with that idea?"

"Well that is the way of it but if she comes in here I don't want you to mention it. I mean it has sure been a mess hasn't it?"

"I will admit sir, strictly in my opinion, there has been quite a bit of disconcert and cacophony on earth as to the implementation of the concept. I don't want to say it was stupid of course and I would never even hint I was thinking such thoughts to Her Majesty But that is my opinion sir."

"Ya, sure has. What was that word you used, 'cacophony'?" Some places the females are all covered head to toe so no one can see em. Other places there are entire dynasties that produce garments designed to show as much of the female as possible without violation of the Hays code. Then there are aromas, lacey things designed to arouse males, and eye goop, and shoes and heels, underwear of silk, lipstick, toe stick, and the derndest holders and fasteners, supports, and secret stuff that even I don't know about. All to make them mysterious, attractive, repellent, lovable, indignant, unflabby, soft, smooth, curvy, with great aroma like an oil pool full of sulphur bacteria and all of that kind of thing. Ya know I really love the smell of sulphur. That is why when her majesty wasn't looking I squirted a bunch of sulphur in the volcanoes and inserted the genes for releasing it in what are called the sulphur bacteria. Or also the solfatera bacteria because the stupid sulphur got joined with oxygen just like the two elements were having sexual attractions and sulphur dioxide would a come pouring out of the volcanoes and just plain sulphur eaters wouldn't know what to do. Sulphur and its various derivative molecules makes things smell so good. Don't you agree?"

"No sir. I mean, truly, yes sir, if you say so."

"Her Majesty said the men would never get excited about legs, arms, toes, curvy soft rear ends, soft titty things, tummies, ears, shaped hips, necks, foots or any of that stuff. Of course it didn't work. There are some women who bind their feet from babyhood to make them very tiny feet, worthless feet, or they put rings around their neck to make them long, or they puncture their tongues, belly buttons, toes, eyelids and put gold rings with amethyst crystals, pieces of broken glass, snail shells, or seashells hanging from their earlobes. I am telling you it was a terrific blunder in my opinion. But now it is done and we have to get along with it. I should have just stopped with binary fission."

"Rabbi Hillel, can I ask you about the Rabbi Hillel thing?"

"If you want. I would probably be more into discussion of why you biologists are so confused about the relationship of my organisms. Why you keep classifying them into two kingdoms, five kingdoms, three domains, eight kingdoms, two empires, all that sort of thing but if you must, ask about Hillel fine."

"When the good Rabbi said 'That which is hateful to you, do not do to your fellow men. That is the whole Torah. The rest is just explanation, go and learn it.' Is that what you intended the whole Torah to say?"

"Pretty much. Not bad for a guy that can't write eh?"

"But there has been so much written by you, so many call it your inerrant word."

"No, not me. Just people that claim it was written by me. I learned my lesson on that early on. Take that Noah story who the writers wrote I hired to run my ark. First they accused me of causing this big rain and flood and wiping everything out. That was not true. That is not the way I do business. Anyway, you know how in the story he builds an ark and floats around for forty days then runs it aground. Next he plants grapes, makes wine, gets plastered in his tent, embarrasses everyone at the party. If you think about it sometime in here the dinosaurs get loose. Now if ya read the scientific literature these animals, that just turn young boys on to the nth degree, lasted for one hundred and sixty million years. Eventually some story teller decided someone threw a rock at the earth and it started a big fire, and changed the gas cover and the big lizards all died. Now I said that just as a metaphor. If someone had really thrown a rock, which no one did, I would hunt down the jerk that wiped out those big birds that were frankly a lot of fun to watch and send him straight to the brimstone pot. It was actually a random event that wiped the dinos out, the kind of thing that happens naturally from time to time. Well, it took a while to get that mess cleaned up and some new things got going that had all had warm blood since that seemed to work fairly good in some of the dinos. The cold blood ones did just fine but I will tell ya they were and still are a god awful crabby bunch that likes to live in swamps. Well time went on, and hominids arose out of these ape things. At some point, I don't remember when, the writers say I met with a guy named Moses. Now I had written a short little simple set of rules for these rather unruly tree huggers to live by and what does Moses do when I give him the stone tablet I carved the rules on. According to the storytellers he gets pissed about his tribe bowing down to this gold image of a cow they made, throws my rules on a rock pile and smashes em to bits. Then has his swordsmen slay a couple thousand kids, grammas, wives, and their men folks. Nothing said in the story they wrote about this about cleaning up the blood and intestines and other innards. Then to make matters worse he leaves, and then writes some rules of his own. These were much longer than what I wrote that is similar to what Hillel came up with several thousand years later. I'll tell you it's just a mess. Would you like another glass of Pinot Noir?"

"Please madam, or I mean sir."

"Think I'll have a half scotch on brimstone this time."

"Ok. So our classification of organisms isn't right yet?"

"No, first there is nothing that is not composed of a lot of other things as well. Would you exist without your consortium of bacteria? No. Would your cells provide energy without their bacterial cells? No."

"Sir, I think I have had enough Pinot for now. I think I might need to go for a walk along the Snake River. I think I need to do a kenosis. Could I come and see you again sometime after I do a kenosis?"

"No problem but I would say you really don't have to do anything like make an appointment ya know. The few, the very few who understand divine immanence, know I enjoy no appointments, no special preparations, no fancy duds, no confessions, confusions, ablations, or blood spills. And I am getting God damn...oops, I am getting real sick of all that fighting and hurting each other, and just being about as stupid as can be that goes on down there, I mean up there, or wherever that blasted ball of suds is now, I keep forgetting where the dumb thing got put. I have got to be more careful too about using that phrase I almost uttered. When you people use it nothing happens. When I use it things like Death Valley come into being. Her Majesty and I lived in the Oasis of the Lushest Palms, California once and I got mad about something their governor did and said those GD words. Presto! Death Valley came into being. Then Her Majesty got dinged off good and we had to move because it was so blank blank hot and I must say the fishing stunk."

"Where did you move to?"

"That's a secret except for guys like you that are not a pain in the ass. For guys like you just remember I am immanent. Ok?"

"Thank you. I will try to remember that. It has been very pleasurable and I might add enlightening to visit with you sir. I just don't know why you keep getting misrepresented so much."

"I don't know either. Her Majesty says I must be patient and let them slowly figure things out. There are a lot who are working on it, so we will just see. Please have a good trip back and I do hope you enjoy more of the wonders right there on earth."

I was pretty tired after my visit with Mr. Dicotyledon. He said quite a bit to make me think hard and when I think hard I get very tired. Sometimes I even get exhausted from thinking so hard and need to take a rest. I figured out some time ago how to make money without doing any regular work, the kind people do when they hoe onions, or lay new asphalt on roads, or sew people up who get their arms chopped up in hay balers, or kicked in the ass hard by a range bull they are trying to put an ear tag on and severely wounded. I am recalling here a guy that got his left rear cheek so badly slashed by a range bull along with some help from a nearby barbed wire fence that he darn near died. He refused to go to any hospital and have his left ass cheek sewed up correctly. He did not want any nurses or doctors or janitors who he thought were all just dying to look at and feel his friggin butt. He said one time they were all a bunch of butt dragons and by god they would not get his. He was unusually bare-butt-phobic I think. Some people are bare-butt-phobic and no one knows why. He was close to dead I learned from a serious infection that developed and made his rear and legs so red and black and full of puss that he passed out and was taken to an emergency room, where they cleaned out the wound and sewed it up and jammed some of the most high powered anti-biotics known to man into his veins. No one thought he would survive it but he did. It was a riot too because more doctors nurses and aides looked at his bare ass than if just one had when it was a simple matter to put in a few stitches. Before it was all through he had had more unholy procedures and practices done than any single man should ever have to endure but it was all his own doing.

I took a rest break to do a kenosis and restore my belief in astronomy. Never the less that night I had another discussion with Starlight.

"One of the things that does not make you mad is astronomy. I don't think I ever got mad at Astronomy. My favorite part of Astronomy is the constellations. Especially the ones that are true. For example in the fall the great flying horse comes surging over the eastern sky with powerful strokes of his wings. It might be her wings. I am not sure if Pegasus is a stallion or a mare frankly. It probably doesn't matter. The thing I like about the big square is I can easily find Andromeda, the beautiful maiden in chains. I tried to write a book about this one time but the dope literary agent I sent it to said she did not deal with dark stories. Shows ya how stupid some literary agents are. She thought this was about some sadistic sex involving maidens in chains. Well the story does deal with a maiden in chains but it is not about darkness it is about light. The whole thing revolves around a Greek myth. Now a myth is a true story that is not true. That is, it is a fictional story about a true trait of hominids that cannot be adequately told by telling a narrative that is true in all aspects. It can only be told by creating fiction which is not literally or historically true or real but that nevertheless gets at the core of reality.

"In the case of the flying horse there is a hero, Perseus by name, who is charged with freeing his people of a problem. It seems there is a trade route where goods and services must pass to the city. There is however a medusa along the trail. Now medusa occur here and there as everyone knows. This one was so ugly that whenever a man looked upon her he immediately turned to stone. Thus all the valiant men sent to get rid of the medusa and restore trade ended up solid rocks. Now Perseus had a leg up on these previous pest control operators. He was born of the Virgin Danae after she was impregnated by the Chief God Zeus who came to her as a cloud of golden raindrops and did the job on her before she even knew what was happening. Well, anyway, Perseus decided to try his hand at ridding the medusa from the trade routes and, this is an important point, he knew he would likely need a better idea than to just go at the medusa head to head with a sword. So he gives the matter some considerable thought."

"While he is doing the thinking it turns out that the queen has done a stupid thing. She has insulted the great goddess of love and beauty. Cassiopea was the stupid vain queen's name and Aphrodite was the beauty goddess. Cassiopea proclaimed she was more beautiful than even the goddess of beauty. Aphrodite was really pissed and of course she did just what you would expect. She orders Queen Cassiopeia's daughter, Andromeda, who had nothing to do with the whole insult, to be chained to a rock where a huge sea monster came each day to feed on fried clams, sautéed octopuses, naughty schoolgirls, and innocent daughters of vain and boastful queens. Even goddesses it turned out could not fire, suspend, or direct air headed queens to be punished or removed from the throne. This, by the way, is a principle that is still in effect today."

"Anyway to return to the story, Perseus being of much higher intelligence than the queen asks the great goddess of wisdom to help him. You can see right off the bat that this is a better way to get started on solving a problem than boasting. The goddess of wisdom whose name is Athena, gives him some help. She has Hermes, the messenger, go to Perseus and loan him his golden shield and some advice. Don't look directly at the medusa or you will turn to stone. Rather, back toward her and guide yourself with the shield looking only at the reflected image. When you are close swing your sword sideways while looking at the shield.

"Perseus does this. He severs the medusa head and while never looking directly at her carries the head to the flying horse that shows up at just the right time. This is the part of the story that frankly is a little hoaky in my opinion. I have rarely if ever had a horse show up just when you need him. So that is the part that seems the most fictionalized. Well Perseus takes advantage of the steed, jumps on his or her back and with the medusa head held behind him flys off into the sky. The horse, having what we now call horse sense, takes Perseus, sword, shield, and medusa to a perfect vantage point over the rock where Andromeda is chained. Just then Perseus spies the sea monster coming to dinner. Spurring Pegasus he swoops down and just as the giant toothed monster is about to devour Andromeda, Perseus plants the medusa head in his field of vision. The monster turns to stone, Perseus severs the chains on the maiden, throws her over the horse, probably gives her a gentle love pat on her gorgeous behind that makes her squeal just a smidgen, then places her behind him on Pegasus. She probably pouts some about this and tells Perseus he is an uncouth bastard but I am sorry I wasn't there and did not get everything that might have been said. Besides there are things that go on between lovers that are or at least should be just between them. That is probably better than some of the overt show and tell that goes on in various places today, even in places like Western Wyoming where you would think they wouldn't or shouldn't. So, off the lovers go into the western sky and live happily ever after.

The end.

Starlight asked, "Do you see a moral here?"

"I do. That is a true story, or an account of reality, that is not historically factual, is not scientifically any thing more than hogwash, defies the laws of physics, chemistry, zoology, evolutionary biology, and the laws of the State of Wyoming. (You are not allowed to hunt medusas in the State of Wyoming without a license that is very expensive and you can only hunt medusas in season. You can shoot just about anything else that lives in Wyoming with or without a license). The Perseus and Andromeda story is never the less a myth that contains within it an eternal truth. It is the kind of truth that is self evident."

"What are you thinking about at this very instance can you tell me that?"

"No. I am thinking simultaneously about the giant dragon flies that arose during the Carboniferous period some 325 million years ago. They were perfect flying machines. They could hover over a pool of greasy water and watch for a tasty morsel of tender baby insect, then break hover, swoop upon dinner, dine, then rocket forward to the females, unite in ecstasy with them in the air, dive, soar, and perform intricate aerial maneuvers of extraordinary delicacy all while enjoying a good screw. You think you and I could pull off a good poke like that in the air? Darning needles do it all. Now here we go again, I am thinking about sex. Every time I try to think about things like the Odonata the next thing that comes up is to think about the dragonflies and the damsel flies and then the word damsel brings up sex and off we go into the wild blue yonder and all you can do is think about getting into some feminine panties if you are a male half of an equation like me. I have no idea what females think about when they think about the Odonata. I am not sure I really want to know if you want the truth.

"I had a reality last night. I was sound asleep when I found myself driving my 13 year old Toyota Camry. I always go on longer trips in my Toyota Camry because it never breaks down. I have even seen Toyota Camrys that are so old they do not look like Toyota Camrys. They are still purring along the highways and by ways with gnomes at the helm. Well, so, here I was along with a bunch of other people some of whom thought they were related to me when suddenly the Toyota that never breaks down, broke down. No matter how much talking I did it would not go. I got out and lifted the hood. There was nothing familiar at all. I mean there was a time in a former epoch, the pre-anthropocene, I believe or the Meat and Potatoes epoch, or maybe it was the Iron, Grease, Timber, and Red Suspenders Epoch. That was when men were men. Now most men still are men so I don't know if that is a good criterion for epochs. Well as you can see I have gotten off track here. I will have a few words about track latter. To get back to last nights reality here is what happened. I was helpless about the stuff under the hood of the Toyota. No one knows how, as in the former epoch, about what to check, what to adjust, what to pull, poke, shake, or tap on with a screw driver. We had no choice but to start walking. Even my cell phone wouldn't have worked even if I had not forgotten to bring it.

"So we start walking. After a few miles we came to what looked like a ranch. It looked more like a Montana Ranch than an Idaho or Wyoming ranch. It takes a long time to tell the difference between these ranch types and usually only an expert, such as the writer of this book, can tell the difference. I would say it was more of a Montana ranch. If I had not forgotten the cell phone I could easily have called up a program that would have answered the question. In fact most people no longer know how to tell these ranch types apart because they never learn how these days. They just use the cell phone to avoid all learning experience.

"Anyway we go through an old buck and pole fence gate and I notice there is a lot of ancient machinery parked all over with tall grass growing through it. There are rusted mowing machines, rusted hay rakes, the kind that used to be pulled by horses, then later IH or John Deere tractors. There were ancient rusted IH and John Deere tractors in the grasses to attest to this. For strange unknown reasons there were galvanized threshing machines, an ancient steam engine with iron wheels, great piles of barbed wire heavily rusted, galvanized water tanks, and many other stupendous artifacts of a by gone age. The machines all retired now reminded me how jobs for people operating these things have also been retired. Now fewer very large machines operated by fast computers do the work of whole hordes of farm and ranch hands. The wealth from the large machines gets concentrated and concentrated.

"There was a very dusty road, pools of oily water, and quite a few bottle flies and horse fly's about. Ya had to watch the horseflies as they were apparently after the blood of any educated white guys that came in their domain today. The horses that were still about the place looked like they had been exsanguinated well before our arrival. Well, finally we get to this pretty dilapidated log house after passing several really dilapidated barns of no particular merit and one shed that had been shot to death from the looks of it. At least there were shell casing all over the dirt and the poor thing had at least several thousand bullet holes in its side.

"At this junction several guys wearing revolvers come out and greet us with both a friendly demeanor while maintaining the option of an all out brawl if need be. I explained the situation as to our presence and they said the first thing I would need to do was to meet Mrs. McWrite who was the owner of the spread. One of the guys then kind of siddled beside me and under his breath asked if I was a teacher. I wasn't sure how to respond so I was honest and said no. It turned out here honesty was good policy as the guy kind of wiped his forehead with a red kerchief and said it was a great relief. He said Mrs. McWrite hates teachers even more than she hates elk and has them taken behind the barn to the south that the north half of the gabled roof has collapsed on and there without further ceremonies has them shot. She has five hands do the job with 1873 lever action rifles that still use black powder. She likes to sit in a rocking chair on the front porch he said and watch the smoke. She especially does not like science, mathematics, or English teachers.

"So I kept saying to myself how prudent I had been in not becoming one of those and of course I probably would not have been able to lie about it and would have been before the firing squad.

"The next thing I knew is that my other passengers had all gone in the house and seemed to be getting along just fine with Mrs. McWrite. No sooner had I determined that Mrs. McWrite still had a copper wire telephone that you could call the neighbors some ten miles up the road than my family came out of a side room, and said Mrs. McWrite had decided to take a nap. I looked in and sure enough she was taking a nap. I was a bit frustrated as I did not know if it was ok to use her phone. I am sorry to report here to any who have read this far into the book that I woke up from reality and back into the dream I sometimes refer to as my regular life. To this day I do not know if the Toyota ever got towed or we got a Toyota trained technician to come and fix it, or what. I know it is really a disappointment to any who just have to know the outcome of every story they read but as I said I do not know what happened."

"So were you worried about this and that is why you have not been in touch with me for several weeks?"

"No, I was only worried about it for two weeks. Then I forgot about it and went to this disrespectable bar and ordered a Pinot Gris. The place was pretty dreary I should tell you and I would not recommend anyone go there. The bartender got to laughing so hard along with a bunch of dudes wearing cowboy boots who were drinking dark amber shots that looked to me like fermented horse piss and then they threw me out. It was better to be thrown out than to get involved with dancing with any of the women who were kind of huddled in a corner. There were guys who were stupid enough to ask one of these women to dance with them at these kinds of bars on Saturday nights and end up with knives in their ribs. I know this is true because I once saw it happen. It is more common in Wyoming ranch country than Idaho ranch country. It may be that in Idaho ranch country more of the ranchers are Mormons and are less likely to start bar fights as they don't want anyone to know they are attending bars on Saturday night but I have not done sufficient research on that to know. I only know not to ask any women I don't know to dance at any Wyoming bars. It is one of the paramount principles I want to get across to you. There are things in this life not to aspire to. Do not ever climb to the summit of any mountain that you do not want to hold in high esteem the rest of your life and do not ever ask a woman you do not know to dance with you in a Wyoming bar."

I keep trying to get all this in order. The trouble is to be an effective writer one must have a melancholic temperament. A melancholic temperament is, according to the ancient Roman physician Galen, a thoughtful and analytic one. This principle that a successful writer needs a melancholic temperament has been authoritatively proclaimed as a universal truth, but I cannot recall who the authority was that did so. It may have been Harumphus. I lean towards a melancholic temperament but I am not very good at it. I have occasions to fall into having a sanguine temperament that is a pleasure seeking type. But being sanguine does not last long. I get over it quickly. Then I slink into being melancholic again. But I stink at being analytical so I usually fall into just being the thoughtful part of melancholic. When I am being thoughtful along comes some phlegmatic type who just stares at me being thoughtful. That sets up a struggle as to which one of us is going to win. I consider becoming a choleric temperament type, which is an ambitious sort and a leader, running for office and passing some laws to make the world work the way I am convinced it should work. But I hate being in power. I hate having the power to decide things for anyone else except me. But that means a lot of people get away with a lot of bad things because with me out of power there are a lot of genuinely choleric people in power who get things screwed up. Unless they are able to see justice and liberty for all clearly and not screw things up. Or at least make progress on unscrewing up things that have already gotten screwed up.

Now there are scientists who are sure this whole temperament type system of Galen based on the Hippocrates theory of humors or bodily fluids that underlie the temperaments is all bunk. Blood underlies sanguine, black bile underlies melancholic, yellow bile choleric and phlegm phlegmatic. This is probably correct. It probably is all bunk. So lets leave it there and move to something else.

"That all seems quite confusing to me." Starlight exclaimed.

"I know. Of course a wise man once said what good is a functioning brain if you don't ever have to use it to navigate your way through a chaotic fog"

"Do you know who the wise man was?"

"It might have been Mr. Eros when he was expounding on love. I suppose, but I just don't really remember.

"You were going to tell me about your loves. You said it was like being in love with two gorgeous wonderful women at the same time and it was driving you nuts. You said you would tell me more about that some time. I think now is a good time," Starlight said.

She had this more or less seductive look in her eye too I might mention. The kind you just don't ignore or brush off with a feather duster. I was going to have to say something here.

"Ok, Let me just tell you about one of the loves. If I can. It is not easy."

"Just relax and tell me about one. Maybe the one you are currently with. In love with that is."

"Ok, Well, drat! One aspect of her is the Greater Yellowstone Ecosystem. Some crazed ecologists now call the Greater Yellowstone Ecosystem the Greater Yellowstone Ecosystem. Now there are women who have all kinds of different personas you know. I think that is what you would call them. Sometimes the same woman wears high heels, a scarf, a pearl necklace, and channel number 9 perfume and drives men nuts. That is what I am saying she looks like in this aspect. She looks like the Yellowstone System. But she does not look the same everywhere. For example, you might look at her in Jackson, Wyoming. Jackson, Wyoming is named after someone whose name I can never remember. Here the woman would be like one climbing out of a Mercedes-Benz that cost $120,000. That, like the price of a house in Jackson, is astronomical, in my opinion that is. It is just too much to pay for a car, a house, or a woman. I recently saw the median price of a house in Jackson Wyoming is over a million. This is not the kind of house one buys to learn about the way the world, the ecosystem, or the ordinary hominid works. One might be able to buy an abandoned refrigerator and live in it but the ones who buy the one million dollar median priced homes have zoned their neighborhoods so abandoned refrigerators cannot be used as homes or laboratories to study the nature of reality, orogeny, or entomology. Nevertheless this is what has happened to one of the loves of my life in this particular aspect of her. This why not much new is being learned about the vicinity of Jackson. It is more or less pickled. I saw this kind of thing happen to my first love too. And it drove me crazy."

"Did you do anything to get over going crazy?" Starlight asked.

"I did a kenosis to dispel notions of wealth being a large house near a ski resort or involving a ski resort in the first place. I did write things down. Among other things I discovered that modern science has pretty much dismissed the ancient notion of the Roman physician Galen that the body humors described by Hippocrates have any validity. I brought that up before as a simple attempt to explain why my writing is the way it is. I do think there is some validity to the ancient concept. I am at divergence with modern medicine and science on this. I do not like being at variance with modern science I can tell you. It gives me the jeepers when I am at variance with such a powerful thing. I think I will let the writing of this exposition on how I got from not so sane to more or less sane speak for itself. I am furtively in turmoil about not being melancholy enough to succeed."

"I suggest you not worry about why your writing is the way it is and just continue your story. You seem to have trouble focusing. Just focus and go forward."

"Alright. Once a long time ago I got myself an old beat up pick-up truck, I started off on an exploration of this little part of the cosmos. It was just called Yellowstone in those days. No body knew much about what Yellowstone was either. It was just a mysterious place of gurgling hot springs, geysers, stinking mud pots, painted pots, and waterfalls. Tourists flocked to it and they sure like the bears. The bears created bear jams of cars, backed up as people saw a bear up close for the first time. I got to admit I fell in love with this new kind of mysterious stuff that was just as alluring as a woman staring at you with wide eyes, the kind of wide eyes when she is attracted to a guy sort of allure. This was shortly after I left my home in search of something. You know what I mean?"

"Yes, I know."

Now I kept a Pulaski in my old beat up pick-up in case its tailpipe or muffler started a grass fire. I drove the old truck around trying to learn what I could. I spent some money on a good pair of binoculars. Well they were not that good but good enough. They had a sturdy strap that wouldn't break and cause you to lose them when ya fall in a mud trap in the Red Rock Lakes National Wild Life Refuge while you are watching the Trumpeter Swans *Cygnus buccinator* the largest of the waterfowl in North America. They also buccinate. Those swans probably buccinate louder and more often than most other waterfowl. The Red Rocks Lakes National Wildlife Refuge is noted for a place where we humans set aside a place for these magnificent remnants of the dinosaurs to continue their kith and kin on an ever increasing man dominated planet. The refuge is located at the upper end of the Centennial Valley more or less at the Southern end of the Gravelly Range. Here one can experience the world in a condition it would be like with out very wealthy anthropocines building houses that have median values way above millions.

"You know what I really liked?"

"Tell me."

"There is sagebrush all over the place. Sagebrush covered country is one of my favorite places to pass through as almost any where you stop there are few other hominids stopping at the same place. Sage brush, by the way, has one of the most distinctive and pleasant aromas in the entire universe.

The aroma of sagebrush is far more alluring than ever a rich woman wore from the scent department of the most expensive scent salons. To the Indians of the sage lands it was sacred. Burned as incense it cleansed the air of bad spirits. If you learn this it is something that helps make you sane when you are losing your grasp on reality. There are, by the way in case you did not know it, three main kinds of Big Sagebrush. There is the tall kind that grows above your head at maturity and for the most part tends to hang along the watercourses. It takes water to grow tall. Then there is the very short Wyoming Big Sagebrush that prefers the much drier, more arid rocky soils of the deserts. In between is found the Mountain Big sagebrush, often on the slopes of foothills. These three Big Sagebrushes all belong to the genus Artemisia named after the Greek Goddess Artemis, the wife of king Mauselaus. All are then named tridentata or *Artemesia tridentata* after their three fingered mitten like leaves. They have summer leaves that they shed and they have winter leaves that they shed. They are the favored place for vesper sparrows to nest, for sage thrashers to thrash, and are on the menu of the pronghorn, the fastest speedster of all the extant North American quadrupeds."

"So this woman you love wears sagebrush #9 and that turns you on?"

"Exactly, Starlight darling."

"Now you are not going to turn me into one of your fantasy lovers, are you?"

"I am trying not to."

"Good, I am just neutral here. Don't forget that! Please continue."

"Do you know not the sense of belonging when walking among the witch hazel?
Do you not understand the harmony of hearing the screech owl speak in the dark?
Have you no communion with the nannyberry in autumnal fruit?
Does not the delicate hepatica send a love note up your spine?

Have you never wondered at the flashes of Photinus in midsummer twilight?
Where is the gentle bluet carpet of the valley floor? Or the August serenade of the katydid?
Have you never missed the whip poor will's plaintive call or the sassafras's' mitten like paw?"

"You do have a lot of strong feelings for those things," Starlight said.

"I often find stopping in the sagebrush a great place to contemplate the superb irrational number e. e=lim k-inf{1+1/k}k. e has been explored by the modern digital computer to trillions of places and remains irrational. If more people understood e there would probably be fewer poor people. If you know a little about it you can use it to calculate interest and the probability of loss at investing or gambling. I am sorry for that repetition. But some things must be repeated. I suppose finding the smell of the universe in the Big Sagebrush deserts of North America is to many a sign of being irrational. Frankly I just don't care. I am on my way to sanity and a little irrationality is usually needed to get to the destination. If there is a destination. As Epicurus advised," just don't care about the destination." Perhaps the nuts that say the journey is the destination are saner and more rational than any who say it is the destination that matters. There are those who have discovered that the place creativity occurs is at the boundary of order and chaos. Too much of either and no creative acts or works result. Once I went just to be in the sagebrush of the Idaho basalt flows. I ran into Mennon Butte, a volcanic tuff wart East of Idaho Falls. Then I wandered into St Anthony Sand Dunes and admired the work of the wind.
Next drove the old beast over Red Rock Pass in the warm season and too much snow in the winter. Then I drove to the Gravelly Range Road and cruised to Black Butte, an ancient volcanic throat that erupted some 28 million years ago. The Gravelly range road will then take you to one of the few places you can drive to a small patch of tundra plants without having to hike uphill. This is not for any lazy bums. It is solely for those who due to some misfortune cannot hike to the alpine on two legs. You can, at the right time in July, see old man of the mountain in bloom. Or sky pilot. You can wander about along monument ridge and see the bright

red sandstones of the Woodside formation laid down in estuaries of the Triassic period. You can walk up Strawberry Butte and see the Permian formation formed when all the continents were joined as one. You could, if you are lucky, be chased back into your battered pick up by a grizzly bear. If you are lucky the bear will not break anything not already broken on your old already badly dented and rickety pick-up. You can continue and descend into the Madison River Valley, where depending on the time of year, you can see many fly fishermen, mostly from far away, many filthy rich, using the most expensive and advance fly fishing technology in the world. The Madison River is, however, still large enough that you can, if you want, still use an old battered bamboo fly rod and a pair of hip boots and a few pale morning duns and catch some nice brown trout. These trout are immigrants from Europe where they are salmon. At least their scientific name has salmon blaring all over it. *Salmo trutta*. Whether they would be allowed to immigrate to the United States today without a lot of political fury, prejudice, restrictions, and regulations is hard to say. If you are going to immigrate to someplace today you need to find a place not already over immigrated to. These places are getting scarcer and scarcer. Once immigrated too and filled with immigrants the immigrants become against immigration.

"So this was all a long time ago. This is a brief description of the love that intruded into my life, and captured my heart. I was still in love with my childhood sweetheart and now this new kind of woman, or whatever it was, had a hold on me. It drove me nuts for a long time as I said before."

Starlight said there was only one way for me to get this split mended and become fully sane. I would have to do a strong kenosis then take a healing journey all around my great love. I would have to look at everything like mountains and put no names on them. I was to just see them as mountains. After that I was to let go of all my prejudices, all my fears, all the thoughts of how things were supposed to be and just let what happened, happen. Of special importance, I had to look at how things are, not the way I might want them to be.

I recorded what happened.

A brief tour of the real world.

One day I shut the door on my small weathered log cabin near Jackson, Wyoming. The cabin was a rarity in the area and had been grandfathered in a low tax zone on a small tract of land where an ordinary citizen could dwell without maxi income. I knew the few of us who still liked simple living were a dying species for this area. Next I found myself actually driving my old hallelujah pick-up truck along the Snake River. I have no real idea how this happened. It just happened. It seems to be spring. The great cottonwoods tell me so in the Psalms of the Cottonwoods. Brilliant yellows of their chlorophyll hidden pigments are invisible now in the light green of the fluttering leaves. Autumn is hidden in those factories. They will in time enough become tired of their labor and desire rest. Then shall autumn burst upon us.

I note the pages of the history of the earth are written in layer upon layer of ancient rocks in the Grand Canyon of the Snake River. Exposed all along the river by the hand of man making his road cut, page after page speaks volumes to the few who can read them. There is a whole chapter on the Permian period when the continents were all united into the great Pangaea some 270 million years ago. I like this page designated as the Phosphoria Formation with its black vivianite mineral seams or phosphorite. Easy reading.

Yea though I walk through the valley in the shadow of life I shall fear no evil for the void is always before me. The moment shinneth within and lights up my soul. The cottonwoods whisper psalms along the roiling waters. A gentle breeze swathes me in peace and I feel I could dwell besides the Snake forever.

Oh, my deep blue eyes! West of the Palisades Dam I see what I thought was a fly fisherman wading the Snake bottom deftly and with focused skill stalking the elusive trouts. But it is not. No, she turns and out of the greenish whirlpool she rises in a mist. It is an angel is it not but it cannot be. I do not believe in angels. No mam. I do not believe in angels. Well except for my guardian angel of course. But guardian angels don't rise from whirlpools in flowing rivers. Of course they don't.

Just to check my brain for malfunction I pull into a roadside turnout, or more accurately, a mud hole along side highway U.S. 26. A Targhee National Forest Entrance sign stands its ground. I read the sign. Brain seems to be ok.

The angel steps out of the swirling river, ascends a somewhat steep bank, and with a sparkle in her eye walks towards my disgraceful old pick-up that has lost much of its paint, has too many dents, has a loose back fender that I should have repaired, and has an oil leak. The leak could be worse I suppose but it leaves a little smudge on the ground when it is parked overnight. The girl, the woman, or the angel, I am not sure which is coming close now. I can see she is really classy. She is both shy and confident. Her face is delicate, soft, and beautiful, beautiful beyond any mortal woman I have ever laid eyes on. I could not be more rankled, more humiliated, feeling more like a failure than at this moment. She must be coming over to look me in the eyes, throw her head back, and without even saying a word dismiss me as no more than a cockroach for owning and neglecting such a disastrously and obviously brutalized 1950s pick-up truck. How could a sane human being, anyone in any semblance of his right mind, be out driving a wreck like the one I was mounted upon, on any road, civilized or not, in the United States of America. No it could not be so in a nation that has any pride and the United States of America, if truth be told, has in general pride, and any one who so abused a 1950s pick-up truck as I obviously had would more than likely be taken up a side canyon by the battered pick up police and shot on the spot.

She, the most seductive, most alluring female figure I had ever laid eyes on, puts her hands on the truck, looks me in the eye and says "Hi. Nice truck."

Around the truck she ambles taking in all its bruises, all its rust, the loose rear bumper, the smell of oil, the slight crack in the windshield on the drivers side, and takes a peek inside the cab where I have carelessly left a peanut butter and pickle sandwich on the seat. Some of the pickle has become unattached and now resides embarrassingly on the cloth itself. This is embarrassing.

"I am Eltanzer." She says calmly but with the utmost authority. "How have you been?"

"I feel like a manure pile." I blurt out.

"Ah, yes." she said more or less under her breath.

Oh, goddamit that did not come out right. "What I meant was my truck feels like a manure pile. No, I am sorry, that is not what I was trying to say either. When I say I feel like a manure pile it means I feel like a manure pile. Drat it all."

I think it was the peanut butter and pickle sandwich thing that got me so confused.

She looks me over but seems very unperturbed.

"You like these Narrowleaf Cottonwoods along the Snake here in the valley don't you? Ah, yes, I see you must call up their binomial Latin *Populus angustifolia*. You are never satisfied with just a common name it must include the binomial. Just like before"

I was a bit taken aback by this knowledge. It was as if this little sprite was reading my thoughts. A scary prospect. I immediately tried to deflect my thoughts to something that would cover up my real thoughts. Just in case she was a mind reader. So I developed the question for her "Are you a sworn dues paying member of the Secret Society of the Sweet Persimmon?"

Before I even completed that thought she said to me, "Of course I am."

"Of course you are what?" I asked.

"A sworn member of the SSSP. The Secret Society of the Sweet Persimmon. The binomial Latin name of the species you are contemplating is *Diospyros virginiana*".

This set me back so hard I fell backwards resulting from not paying attention to a stick that had fallen from a narrow leaf cottonwood *Populus angustifolia* and I crashed onto my highnee. Or is it hyney, hiney, or hi-knee? I could not get the spelling correct as I sat there on my hinee. This was truly a dangerous situation as I was completely stunned and felt unsure about how to defend myself against someone who seemed right out of an advanced Brave New World that could read thoughts. I wondered if all this stuff that has been rampant on the news networks about the NSA developing advanced computation tools that can break just about any codes, could maybe perhaps have developed a way to pick up brain waves, decode them, and implant them into one of their advanced agents in the field. Here I was, just a lowly, very lowly biologist in a direct confrontation with big brother. Or big sister, it could even be something big like 1984 Orwellian takeovers by tyrants with thought police had happened and I had missed it due to being absorbed in wandering the western forests enjoying learning's about plants and trees. I had been sifting through ancient geological formations looking for some new piece of evidence that might be of scientific value. I had been, on occasion, enjoying a glass of a fine Pinot Noir from the Columbia River vineyards that had been reduced in price enough for me to afford it and taste the gout de terror of what I was convinced the finkyest French connoisseur would approve of the ancient and venerable work that the lowly yeast *Saccharomyces cervisiae* had wrought on the purple fruit of the grape.

"I love the Pinot Noir too; the sumptuous lips on the beautiful face informed me."

"That pushed me hard. She was definitively an advanced agent reading my brain waves as I had said not a peep about enjoying the fruit of the vine."

"I do also adore the Pinot Gris." she whispered.

That was it, final proof of her tuning into not only my current thoughts but also my memory banks as I had not been thinking of the Pinot Gris at all but after the Pinot Noir it is my next favorite. I will tell you I was in a place of *extemis*, worried, wondering, astonished, amazed, but most strange of all not the least bit scared. I should have been scared but I wasn't.

We left the pullout by the Snake and drove along U.S 26. I cannot tell you how this happened. One just does not drive off with a stranger who happens to be a female, who happened a few moments before to be wearing fly fishing waders, who seemed to be a mind reader, who was clearly an agent of the new world order, and who just got in the passengers side of my abused pick-up truck and somehow avoided the peanut butter sandwich mess. It was mind blowingly incredulous how she avoided sitting on the peanut butter and pickle sandwich.

I could give you intimate details about which roads we traversed during the day and whether we obeyed the speed limit or not or had a flat tire but these are not of much cosmic weight or of much pertinence. One road was marked Idaho 33 if you must know. It climbed over a pass that not too many know about. Pine Creek Pass. Massive Cretaceous age rocks were tilted almost vertical and were colored in a whole palette of colors. I wish the Cretaceous had just stuck with one kind or maybe two kinds of limestone or sandstone or sand but no it had to be multi colored, multi textured, multi just about everything and had the largest dinosaurs ever, and also framed the demise of the big ground lizards.
I was thinking about Tyrannosaurs when I was interrupted by Eltanzer.

"I suppose I could have asked if it was ok for me to ride along with you on this grand scheme you are undertaking." she purred.

"How do you know about my grand scheme?"

She created a sassy smile that told me she knew. She knew!!! She Sassafras knew!!!!!

"I believe you will tell me about your grand scheme. You will tell me about it won't you?"

"Only if I feel like it. Maybe if I Fig Newton."

"I make you nervous, don't I? And you lose it. You get into such a funk and say, 'maybe if I fig Newton.'"

"I do not!! And you cannot come with me. I don't even know who you are! You are some kind of hussy. That is it. You are a hussy and you are going to seduce me and get me to pay you. Then you will steal my wallet while I am exhausted. You cannot come with me. No sir! No man! No mam, I mean. Absolutely not! I am not that kind of man. I do not pay hussies for a little nookie. You probably want me to just take everything off and then we do it, and then you collect your booty, and put your bra and panties back on and then I suppose you get me to get out of my truck and look at what you said is a funny noise on your side of the truck. Then poof you jump in the drivers seat, put her in gear and off you go with my truck, my pants, my wallet, and my jar of peanut butter."

"Oh, you are such a fig Newton."

"I suppose you are aware that I am an Epicurian, I place an inordinate value on friends. I especially place value on friends who I can speak my mind to and say the wrong thing to, or something stupid, or something that does not come out right, and they remain my friend. They will even let me correct a mistake without prejudice."

"Of course, I know all about that. Do you remember the time you read from Ralph Waldo Emerson what he said about friends? That 'a true friend was someone before whom he could think out loud.'" You were really impressed by that."

"Yes, I was. Darn flub it."

"And you enjoy pleasurable things such as looking for fossils, learning plant names just because they are beautiful, savoring a fine Pinot Noir, hearing a chickadee discuss chickadee philosophy with you from the snow covered boughs of a spruce tree, staring at Coma Berenices in the spring sky, and feeling a connection with the ancient Greek philosophers. These and many other pleasures are your milieu. And it is no coincidence that you have little ambition to become powerful, or wealthy, or famous. In fact you adore being anonymous, a face in the crowd, non distinct. Just as Epicurus said was the best way to live. No fear of any future judgments and punishments, no worries about eternal torture in lakes of brimstone scorching the skin, or flagellations tearing the flesh. No, just dissipations of your hydrogen and carbon, your oxygen, sulphur, and nitrogen back into the great void."

"You see those hills over there?"

"Yes, what are they?"

"The west side of the Teton Range. The Grand Tetons. The one with the cute little sort of knob on top sort of reminds me of female things interesting to guy things."

"There looks to be three of em, to me."

"The French called them Le trios tetons. I think this is the vantage where they got that idea. Most people don't see them from this side so don't understand."

"You like Tetons? Oh how dumb of me, of course you like tetons. You can stare at mine if you want. Just keep hands off. While you are driving at least. Maybe later, if you are a good boy, I will let you fondle them. Just a little."

The thought the mere thought of fondling her delicious tetons made my jeans hard. I would have to stop and throw this sassy sassafras out of my truck. It was to distracting to argue with her, to even think of fondling the tops of those mountains. It was the craziest darn thing. I must be going nuts. I would ditch her at the Teton River. Some lunatic fisherman would pick her up and pay her for her services and then dump her in Teton Idaho where she could do little harm. I suppose little harm.

"Some abandoned Dairy farms passed through the windows. Cows once grazed here making pasture fed milk. The kind that is healthful. Has Omega 3 fat in the milk and cream."

"Where did they go?"

"Now the dairy cows and their fabulous Tetons are gone from the Teton Basin. They are jammed into industrial operations along the Snake. Horrendous!"

We cross the Teton River and ascend a small rise. The magnificent river meanders through willow forests and still harbors cutthroat trout. I am fantasizing about fondling Eltanzer, who has somehow managed to show substantial bare thigh as her silky skirt has worked its way skyward towards her slender waist and her stunning Tetons. My plan to ditch her at the Teton Bridge falls apart. It would be un-gentleman like. And I am a gentleman. I think if I just stroked her inner thigh a little bit with the tips of my fingers it would not disqualify me as a gentleman. Nor would it incur a large monetary indebtedness. "Your honor, I just touched her bare thigh very briefly, a very light touch mind you, not the sort of thing that one usually pays a fee for. Surely you will not fine me or require payment in equity, or anything like that. Will you? Your honor."

We pass from the rural pastures into a beehive, a bustling mass of cars, traffic signals, buildings and businesses everywhere. Swarms of hominids occupied crosswalks. I drive to the top of the hill on which a dazzling white structure reminiscent of a mausoleum dominates the hilltop. The Rexburg Temple. A single steeple in the central tradition of the modern Mormon faith sported the golden angel Moroni blowing a horn. Inscribed on the glowing alabaster architecture is written.

Holiness to the Lord

The House of the Lord

"I have long been interested in the Mormon faith," I said. "Because it arose in my native land in the New England of the 1830s, a time of intense religious fascinations." Moroni was the angel who appeared unto Joseph

Smith, the prophet, and showed him the golden plates buried on the hill Coumorah in western New York. Written in strange hyroglyphics Joseph Smith translated the texts using a seer stone. The result of his work was the Book of Mormon, an addition to the traditional Bible of the Christian faith. There were many new additions to the Christian faith such as God being the first man, the celestial marriage, and the doctrine of elevation or of the faithful practitioner becoming a god himself and, in an afterlife, ruling over his own planet. Smith in a vision had seen both God and son Jesus in a vision in the eastern woods. They were to him separate persons in human form. Eventually at just age 39, Smith was murdered in Nauvoo Illinois. These untimely ends seem to happen quite frequently to people who start new spiritual systems. That is why I have never applied to start any new religious systems."

"Yes I know of your interest in how religious systems begin and your avoidance syndrome."

"It still absorbs my attention that founders of faiths have these encounters with angels who impart to them 'revealed knowledge.' Was this not the case when the angel Gabriel gave the Quran to Muhammed? Yes. Was it not also the case with father Abraham in the Mesopotamian desert? With the annunciation in the gospel of Luke regarding the birth of Jesus?"

"Yes, those all were guided by those incorporeal beings, usually winged messengers of a supernatural God. Now the wings have been around ever since Hermes, also known as Mercury, showed up in the Greek pantheon. Mercury was unabashedly the messenger of whatever god needed to mail some instructions to lowly mortals."

"So even here, in the modern country, that just over the horizon from our present location, still maintains a vast research laboratory that has explored the nuclear structure of the atom, made it practical for submarines and other naval vessels to operate on atomic power, remaining submerged for months at a time, to study such newer interests such as how Archea get along in the hot acidic volcanic pools of the Great Yellowstone Caldera. Yet still angels rise among us."

"Aren't you going to take me in the temple?"

"You know very good and well I am not. We are not allowed. Besides it says somewhere the Lord is not in temples."

"Yes, You have struggled with that for a long time. And it is indeed written."

The God who made the world and all that is in it,
The Lord of heaven and earth does not dwell in sanctuaries
made by human hands.

"It is written? You just know that stuff my darling Tanzer? Where is it written as you so succinctly just stated?"

"Why it is written in the book of Acts Chapter 17 verse 24."

"Darn it all. I can never recall chapter and verse like that when I need it. How do you do that? I feel so humiliated by you Eltanz. Like I am riding with an encyclopedia that knows all kinds of stuff. What I am thinking in my deepest recess. I hope you don't know everything. I hope you do not know the, the------"

"The odd little sexual thoughts you are now harboring. The ones you hold secret in your imagination. The ones that make you get hard, fast?"

"It worries me. It worries me you know about those too. And you play with me. You tease me, and I am scarred I cannot resist you. I am afraid I will surrender to your charm, your magnet that pulls me like iron filings into your chamber and you pleasure me with relentless abandon."

"I am having a good time." Eltanzer said.

We leave Rexburg and continue soon back in the sage lands of the Snake River Plain.

"What is that?"

"They are called the Menan Buttes. North one is Called North Menan Butte, South one is called South Menan Butte. They are cool. They are volcanic cones that formed in the Pleistocene when they boiled up from the earth into a fresh water lake. They hardened into a frothy kind of mess called tuff."

"I wonder how many people drive down the interstate highway not far to the west and never know what they are, perhaps never even notice them?" she pensively said.

"I don't know but they are unlikely to be Epicurians."

"I like them. And there is the right number of them."

"I see you have changed. I see you are now wearing high topped boots with a little bit, not too much, of a heel, not those long black spikes that some women don to convert themselves into a dominatrix or make them taller or whatever. No, yours are just the right kind. I see you have changed out of those fishing waders into a skirt. I see the skirt is rather tight around your waist and makes you look almost irresistible. Your sparkling wide eyes are so damnable alluring I am losing the power of concentration in my mind. I am supposed to practice focusing on single thoughts. Tanzer darling, you are making it almost impossible for me to focus on a single thought except for one over whelming, very strong and powerful thought. I think they call it lust. According to some ancient philosophers it was a deadly sin. We were not supposed to have those thoughts. But as far back as I can remember they would just come up. Tanzer, my love, I am going through this to divert my attention from your utterly, impossibly alluring being. Oh, my god, did you have to cross your legs like that and pat your knee with your fingers in such a delicate feminine way. I am now thinking about how to prune grape vines so they will bear more fruit. Darn it. I love grapes. They taste so sweet and good and that reminds me how sweet and good holding you tight would be. I would even be inside you. A little bit at least, if not all the way. I could hold on to your soft bannock buns while I was inside you a little bit. Not too far of course just a little bit. Not enough to be considered un-gentleman like."

"Try thinking about something not Epicurean. Will you try that just for me?" Eltanzer whispered.

I had to do something. I just had to somehow divert my whole nervous system from being the wild animal it was on the verge of becoming. Ah in about 680 CE Muhammad's cousin, Ali, husband of his daughter started a long-standing rift in Islam, the Sunni/Shiite rift. Hussein was his name, and no relation to a president of same, and he got in a fight with a rival Caliph at Karbala. Hussein and some seventy two of his followers stood their ground but lost the fight. Hussein was beheaded. Now here is the part that may be my needed ice water. Those who survived him and became his followers, some of them at least, and continuing to this day, took up a ritual of self-flagellation to commemorate his martyrdom. These rituals were not invented by or confined to Muslims either. Many of the early Christian saints practiced the infliction of pain on themselves with whips, straps, or chains, to imitate the scourging of their Lord and savior.

"Hm, good. Are we cooling off now?"

"Yeah that last crazy crud is working, like jumping in a salt water hole in the arctic ice. Very chilling, very chilling. Ok, I think it is just like a wet charcoal log now. Like in a campfire one is leaving. " I rather gruffly said.

This only made Eltanzer laugh.

"I forgot to ask." She said, "Would it be ok if I circumbabulate the Greater Yellowstone system with you. And when we are done you can drop me off in Jackson?"

"You live in Jackson?"

"I did not say I live in Jackson. I said you could drop me off in Jackson. Maybe before if we are done."

My God, the princess was going to drag out of me why I was doing this preposterous journey. That just more or less got me infuriated. I would resist her in my opinion. Just to show how in control of myself I was. I would show this Venus a thing or two.

At this point, Johnny Cash's crooning with June Carter came crashing out of my auditory data storage area. 'We got married in a fever' and something about peppers, and Jackson but I think it was another Jackson and I got confused about the meaning of life all over again. What a mess. All I wanted to do was drive my poor old Chevrolet just once around the Yellowstone caldera before the poor bastard blew out its head gaskets, dropped its drive shaft, turned off its lights, spilled all its motor oil on the ground and commenced its journey into iron oxide. There are a lot of things in addition to fabulous pickup trucks that eventually get oxidized into the elements of the earth, the elements of the universe. Some of the elements in our bodies up to iron were manufactured by our local star we call the sun. Some came from long past stars that died in unimaginable explosions that made elements heavier than iron. But these too will oxidize and even though they are immigrants from distant parts of the universe will no doubt be allowed to remain on Earth without exceeding their VISA. Most were of course grandfathered in and no visa was required in the first place and no acts of congress or adjudications by immigration bureaus or supreme courts were involved either.

All of this did help a little but not like it was a permanent cure or anything. I mean I was suddenly recalling the bugling elk of Grand Teton National Park around Signal Mountain and all the meadows of the great Teton front in October when the cool air, the changing slant of the sunlight, the full growth of fighting weapons on their magnificent heads, and some interior chemicals we refer to as hormones brought these ungulates into frenzied attraction to the lovely cow elks who apparently enjoy watching the great bulls compete sometimes violently for the attention of the lovely ladies. We believe the ladies even emit chemicals of their own that signal the bulls their willingness to allow the strongest defender of his territory and his harem to find relief from the great tension such as I have been trying to dispel. What I am trying to get to here is my utter admiration and sinful envy for the elks, the deer, the pronghorn, and other members of the bovids who can spend the majority of their year feeding on sumptuous plants, wandering about the plains, mountains and meadows, identifying plants, taking in vast panoramas of mountain splendor and not have to deal with the allure of their harems. They can think about eternity, think about infinity, and have no interrupting thoughts or desires or need to fight for the privilege of sticking their joy stick in the soft gushy chasm of a female elk. Those lucky smucks can get it all over in a month or so, a tremendous blowout of those terrible desires and the combat for who gets who. A little rest from the tasks that virtually exhaust the poor patriarchs of future generations, and then a year of not being greatly concerned about it.

"Do you mind if I come with you? You did not say before."

Oh this was going to be trouble, or at least difficult, or perhaps sublime. I was after all trying to decide if being sane meant living in fear of the wrath of a supernatural god as a large number of my countrymen hold to be the true reality, or if I needed to be prepared to live forever as a god myself, or perhaps as those who believe in "theosis" believe a long long journey of becoming godlike. The other option was to accept that upon death, I would soon be reduced to basic elements whether by the flame of the crematorium or the action of bacteria, fungi, and perhaps other organisms. No divine judgments, no eternal tortures if I came up short of some divine laws or principles, just absolute nothingness, total emersion in an unconscious void, never to resurrect again as a sentient thinking being.

Now if that was not enough to overwhelm my thought processing center I had a flashback to an earlier overwhelming event. There I was in an eastern swamp in the Autumn when the sugar maples were shimmering orange and the red maples were scarlet beyond my understanding. It might have been along the Alleghany or the Susquehanna, or it might have been the Delaware, the Pequest, or the Paulinskill, I couldn't exactly place it. There were throughout the landscape many of these stands of maples that left an indelible imprint and stirred the soul in the great eastern forest phantasmagoria of autumn. I missed it all in my heart, like a lost love and suddenly it hurt something fierce.

I shook off the fantasy to put a stop to the heartache.

She was so alluring; I was so taken with her I knew despite my better judgment what I would say.

"Of course you can't come with me. You know very good and well I cannot take you with me. There really could be nothing good come of it. I am trying to tell you I don't think this thinking about something else will work every time for me to keep my paws off of you, darling. Do you? There is only so much a guy like me can do to stand up against the great provocative power of her majesty to unite, to procreate in the embrace of pleasure. Tanzer, darling sweetheart, have you never gazed at the great painting by Sandro Botticelli who, in my uneducated, non art connoisseur opinion, is a spectacular rendition or her majesty's brilliance. The graces, Beauty, Chastity, and Pleasure, dancing among Flora's spring flowers while Venus looks on with apparent satisfaction and the little god Eros aims his bow at Chastity. I think the little prick is aiming his bow at you right now and I do not know what to do."

"Thank you. I am glad you will let me ride with you. It sounds like a lot of fun. And I will be a big help to you. I can change a flat tire you know. I am a good map reader so I can help navigate. I have some money, not a lot but if we have to stop and get some vittles I can help. And I know about good nutrition. I am up on the latest research about healthy eating."

This was going to be harder than I thought. I could not remember if I said "No, definitely not, You can not come with me. Absolutely not." or if I said "definitely!" But now I couldn't just stop, walk around the truck, open the passenger door and order her to get out. I could not leave this gorgeous angel along an American rural road out in the sagebrush. She might be picked up by a crazed animal in an old battered pickup and taken advantage of. I knew this sort of outrage happens. It is one of the most cowardly things done by male humans. Some do not know the natural law. They do not know like the elk do that the female must choose who she will allow into her mysterious realm of pleasure. The bull elk must win her not force her.

"This muse in my battered pickup had decided something, I could tell. She had decided to come along with me whether I liked it or not. So I said "Ok, I will let you ride with me a while. I can't just leave you out here in the sagebrush."

"Yes, you can!"

"No, I cannot do that. It would be too dangerous for the sagebrush. And don't tell me what I can do."

"Oh, you know you like being told what to do sometimes. It is a lot easier than deciding you know. But for now I won't tell you what to do. For now. Later I might tell you exactly what I want you to do and I can assure you will obey me."

"I will not.

I was head over heels in love with Eltanzer. Already. And it was just starting to be the end of the first day. I have heard about this kind of calamity. Love at first sight. I of course did not believe in it. It was not rational; it was just not something that was supposed to happen. I was not even sure what it meant to fall in love, let alone at first sight. But what I was now experiencing brought up the question. Did I not believe in love at first sight because it never happened or was it because I was taught it never happens? I knew I was taught it never happens. But that teaching was now in conflict with the fact that it was now happening. I knew I was rational, all the time, but this was a cognitive dissonance of the first order. If I still smoked a rosewood pipe I would have filled the bowl with fine burley tobacco, lit the thing, made some spectacular puffs, and given the matter some serious thought. I gave up smoking the pipe because science had demonstrated with sufficient probability that tobacco use in any form is too much associated with anti epicurean joys of life such as cancers of the lung, mouth, throat, colon, all other organs, heart disease, breathing diseases, and also even annoys others who do not like blue clouds of exhaled smoke in confined spaces. It shortens the ephemeral flowering of life, makes time of the shortened period often fraught with pain, and I believe is not allowed in heaven either at least the one the believers believe in. That includes the heaven the believers in supernatural heaven believe in and the one that they don't believe in which is the one right here on the planet Earth. Do not get me going on that Tanzer, sweetheart. Just leave it be.

I just kept driving, keeping my focus on the white lines of the road. I decided to stay in the vicinity of Saint Anthony's Sand Dunes a bit north of Rexburg, Idaho. There were sagebrush lands along the way to keep my prurient interests a little bit at bay, not much, or enough but a little bit. There were juniper trees along the way. These managed to help with subduing my prurient problems a little more than the sagebrush since I had forgotten how to tell the Rocky Mountain Juniper apart from the Utah Juniper and that annoyed me to no end.

"I read the other day one can tell the difference between Utah Junipers and Rocky Mountain Junipers by the number of seeds in the berries. Utah has one while Rocky Mountain has two, usually."

"Did you know the Rocky Mountain Juniper has its male flowers on one tree and its female flowers on another?" Eltanzer the mysterious rider informed me.

This more or less got me a bit perturbed. She was obviously trying to seduce me by clearing the obstacles I was placing in the path she was drawing me down. I set my jaw and kept on going. It was getting towards twilight when I looked to my right and could see in the evening light off to the eastern horizon those three curious peaks, the summits of the Grand Tetons with Grand Teton looking exactly like the shape of one of the grand tetons adorning the Grace of Beauty riding in my truck. The angle she was magnificently holding her upper torso also produced a nice lovely replica of the next Teton on the horizon. This only reconfirmed my hypothesis that the French fur trappers who were responsible for naming that great range had in fact gotten it most right Darn stuff just keeps recurring, can't get away from it.

We pulled into a campsite in full view of the St Anthony Sand Dunes that had a wonderful soft glow in the twilight. Not widely known, these sand piles seem to have accumulated from wind borne sands blowing from the Snake River Plain and dropping them, sand grain by sand grain, and pushing up crescents in the existing pile of tiny little white quartz bits into awesome barchan dunes.

I will spare the reader from the mundane chores of setting up a camp, of cooking some stew I managed to remember to bring along that I cooked in my iron Dutch oven stove pot that was quite black, and a few other preparations for the night. I came up with a bottle of Pinot Noir from the Oregon grape country, and while the sun set we enjoyed the bouquet and palette delight with one of the muses of old.

It was a dark enough night that the stars came out quite brilliant. It was the time of year when Vega the brightest star in the summer sky rose in the East in the constellation Lyra. And of course to my unnerving Venus would be hanging in the Western sky as the evening star. Of course.

Eltanzer told me of the story of St Anthony who I supposed the dunes were named after. I was a little dim on the history of Saints as I was not raised in a religious system that considered saints as anything more than idols, worshipped by prevaricators and perverters of the true religion.

"Saint Anthony lived from 251-356 Ad. He was known as Saint Anthony of the Desert because he wandered in the Desert of Egypt that was of course a great wilderness. In this place he called a primordial landscape he felt he attained an absolute connection to the divine. When he returned to more civilized places he thought the devil was against him and beat him while wild beasts attacked him.

So he returned to the desert, found an oasis since no human can long survive without water and became an ascetic. He was not left alone as people searching for something kept coming to him thinking a hermit out in the desert had some special open line to God and they wanted to hear what God had to say. 'Get rid of the possessions he probably told them. Be kind to the poor, Live a simple life'," she said. Then her grace decided she was tired. Off came the boots, off came the skirt, and off came the tankard or whatever you call those tops.

I don't know where she came up with it but she pulled a kind of night gown on, and slipped into a sleeping roll. I had for reasons unknown to me two of them in the tool box. I don't remember putting two in the box but there were two in the box. I crawled into mine as well. I was relieved that she had decided not to further test my powers of thinking about something else. I, for example, had decided that I would never get married. Well at least I had decided that I would never engage in sex with a live breathing female unless I was ineffably bound to her as husband and wife. I had promised my self that I would not do that. No promiscuous fooling around by me I had promised. It was just me that had promised that to me. No other humans, no other gods, no god of the secret spying version so prevalent in my country's dominant culture, the one who sees everything and knows everything, even knows more and sees more than the vaunted sergeants of the U.S. Marine Corps, one of whom had informed me that they see all, know all, and do all. Yes mam, this was a promise I made to myself, to my mind, to my body, to my soul, the life force that dwelled within me. None of this had anything to do with the legal institution of marriage that is just a social structure established by law. I had kept my promise too. I knew I had no foreign immigrants in my body also. I had no *Neiseria*, or *Vibrio*, or Treponema spirochaets, viruses, or Chlamydia, or fungi or behemoths that would ever attack my immune system, lay me low in horrible misery, put me in the ground before a good adventure through paradise. None of that for me except of course the normal auto release of fluids that our biology dictates must be expelled. And I never confessed this expulsion to any confessors because it was not something that needed to be confessed about. It was ordained by Her Majesty, it was necessary even to the development in the psyche for one day being selected by one of the muses to mate with her, to be in a marriage or lifelong partnership with her, a friend of the greatest depths, and one who I could say "I am all yours". I was hoping the muse who selected me might also have made the same kind of promise to herself. I knew from many temptations it was a supremely difficult promise.

In the morning we walked on the dunes, we bared our feet so to feel them as well as see them. We looked from the top down the wavering slip side where sand from the ridge moved gently down the crescent. We knew we were looking at something that was just ours for a sand dune never stays the same.

With the important work of enjoying the sand dunes taken care of I decided to veer a little off course in my great circumnabulation of the Yellowstone Caldera. I drove past the Camas National Wildlife Refuge where some tundra swans were resting on their northern migration in the cattail marshes we have cleverly decided to set aside. In these places, mostly too small, the remaining migratory waterfowl rest and refuel. These living descendants of the dinosaurs still migrate from the Arctic regions in the fall to places where open waters exist then back in the spring to build nests, make love, and rear future generations.

The next place we came to was striking in its dark bleakness. Black rock piles, made of basalt, cropped up. Eventually we entered a place of dark cinders. The names of these cinder heaps is "spatter cones" for the steeper ones and "craters" for the less steep. They are the remnants of volcanic eruptions from the Great Rift that crossed south central Idaho. They are along but probably not related to the track of the Yellowstone caldera that extends from Southeastern Oregon to its present residence in Northwestern Wyoming. Of course those addresses did not exist during the caldera eruptions along an arc starting about 16-17 million years ago and last blowing its lid about 639,000 years ago. There are great arguments about whether the eruptions along the track result from deep vertical plumes of magma deep in the lower mantle of the earth or are the result of upper mantle geological processes. The black cinder cones are a thorn in the side of the believers in the deep magma hypothesis as they erupted only 15,000 to 2,000 years ago according to the geologists who have investigated them.

I did not come here to resolve the matter as I am not a well enough experienced geologists to argue the merits. What I wanted to show Tanzarita was the strange little white spots that dot some of the barren craters of black cinders. They are covered with white spots like chickenpox of lava cones.

I found myself holding her hand as we climbed up a trail. It was probably a good thing the National Park Service had made a few trails so people would not trample all over the place. They might have done harm to the white spots for here growing out of what appears a lifeless, waterless, barren of plant food, heap of cinders is a little buckwheat that has found a way to make a living.

"I have never seen such a courageous being." she purred obviously quite impressed with the matted plants that found a way to not only survive but appear to thrive on this alien landscape.

"It is not called 'Craters of the Moon' for its lushness." I managed to get out in an attempt to sound knowledgeable and important.

Being a little sassy she said, "I suppose the entrance sign that said 'Entering Craters of the Moon' was not an influence on your diagnosis. I am fairly sure I read someplace that no water was discovered on the moon."

Frankly, the way she said that with this sparkle in her eye, this little taunting of my masculine pride and that sort of crap made me want to kiss her, or pat her rear, not hard of course, just the kind that says I am head over trash barrel in love with you. Or at least give her a good verbal dressing down. Trouble arose in my psyche again, as you would expect.

"The Latin name of this plant is *Eriogonum ovalifolium* var depressum". I said, with an air of authority.

"That is a stupid name," Tanzer the The Sun Ray growled. How could so courageous, so beautiful a little being be named depressum. These little sweethearts are the polar opposite of depressed."

This brought me out of my little, very minor, not significant funk. "I must agree with you, it is a botch up. There are times I do get mad at the rules of taxonomy and for the dopes who would goof up a plant's name like this. Tell you what. I am taking down a note to commence a campaign right here and now to get that fixed. I will not win of course but it seems a worthwhile endeavor. There are things like this that need fixing. So even though it is of course, utterly hopeless, I am starting right now a campaign. What should I propose as a replacement?"

"I like *Eriogonum ovalifolium* var silenensis for their love of the moonscape," my new found love brought forward. "You do know 'Selene' is one name for the goddess of love I believe."

"I do."

My jumping kangaroo rats, those words scared me. That is what is said at weddings and I, to date a bachelor and crazy person, and way too poor in wealth, power, money, career potential, stability, a botanist to boot and an admirer of bugs, a sifter of dirt, and believer in enjoyment of learning, could most likely, in my opinion, not be involved in what has become known as marriage in the land of Vespusio Americi. Marriage was an economic unit that confined people to cells in suburbs of large urbanized masses that had plenty of people all competing for the right to spend as much money at the Temple of the Invisible Hand. The invisible hand had for some time visited the planet and was guiding every sane human into sacrificing their labor, their minds, their creative works, everything to make stuff, buy stuff, and throw it away so more stuff could keep flowing in the great spiral called the world economy. The gravity of the system had now consolidated the actual wealth, that is the power to control the flow, and what the people did, and what the people worshipped, into dense low populations of a few men. That is what gravity does. It takes hydrogen atoms and collects them into swirling clouds, then into dense clouds, then into thermonuclear reactors that release immense quantities of energy and particles into the cosmos. Eventually the stars use up the hydrogen they have collected. They either flicker out in a kind of ember or, if they are big enough, they explode. The power of the explosions makes new elements that are hurled into the universe and end up being re-incorporated into other stars and other solar systems. So in the end it does not matter who started the whole thing, which controlled the whole thing, or what they made. It all comes to an end. That is what happens on the earth in the economy. And today the giant crush of social gravity is tearing at a very fabric of the human heart, the idea of a long and lasting friendship we

used to call marriage. Now we know those words "I do" for so many, are
an entry into a great suffering, a great loss of happiness.

"Do you understand Mr. Proud Bachelor that marriage is just a legal
matter? It has nothing to do with the ineffable bond between a husband
and a wife. That bond exists way beyond any of the social conventions
called marriage. It is even the case in the great genesis story of Adam and
Eve. Nowhere does it say Adam and Eve were married. It just says they
were husband and wife."

"Tanzer, Tupelo. You kill me with stuff like that."

I was driving east again, out of the moonscape, along Idaho 22 a paved
road. I was wondering if I had helped pay for the construction of the road.
I hoped so. I do not like free loaders. I really wanted to have the dignity
of knowing I helped finance the road. We arrived at I-15. I was relieved. I
knew this was a federal road and I had paid federal taxes both to the IRS
and to the road builders at the gas pump. Knowing I was about to use the
interstate I told the beautiful Tanzer I would just drop into the gas station
and fuel up and pay a little towards my obligation to maintain the federal
highway. After filling up the poor old battered beast of burden made of
iron mostly derived from our own sun, I decided to have a quick look at
the local town, Dubois, Idaho. Tanzer had a bit of a frown, a sorrowful
countenance, as we went into the heart of Dubois. The place appeared
to have suffered from a serious plague. Buildings were very sick, old, not
cared for. Businesses were closed. The Rasmussen Hotel and an old brick
building called the Meeker Block slept in a kind of death pallor. "A ghost
town in the womb," was the diagnosis of the lovely sprite in my pickup.

We drove north on I-15, observed the distant Lost River Range, then
started a climb. We passed through Spencer that claimed it was the opal
capital of the world.

"That is impressive," I informed Tanzer. "The whole world and we are in
its opal capitol. You like fire opals my darling? Perhaps I should stop and
acquire one for your pretty neck. Maybe you would swoon into my arms
and paradise would flash from your eyes and dance in the fire opal."

"I rather like the block signal," she said.

"I like the fire opals. They were made millions of years ago by geysers. The best ones sparkle with red, green and blue flashes especially in the sunlight," I informed my traveling sprite.

She is a strange one I thought. A cute, gorgeous, sweet, strong, and powerful female who could probably walk in a motion picture studio and get a million dollar part any day of the week, is impressed by a black block signal on the only Union Pacific Railroad line that incurs into the State of Montana. It is a single track line most of the time and I wonder why block signals are required. They only run three trains a week. But I have to agree with her. Block signals are cool. They remind one of the complexities of running iron monsters on iron rails. Monsters that are so fuel efficient compared to the trucks and battered pickups on the interstate. The rails use so little land compared to the interstate. I was mulling all this over when I glanced at Eltanzer. She had now taken her top off and was wearing only a black bra that was most cunning in its ability to hold her grand tetons in a ravishing pose. She had decided to let her hair, which had for the past few hours been piled on top of her head, now hang low covering her delicious shoulders. I wondered how she could have such a tight waist, no belly fat, everything just primp and plum.

"What are those trees?" she asked.

"Those are peaches," I blurted out.

"Quit it." She scolded. You want me to just slap you or something."

I worked my way around the fog my mind was in. I glanced at the trees now adorning the hills, hills that were in the Targhee National Forest.

"Those are interior Douglas Firs *Pseudotsuga menziesii* var glauca" I got out. And the proof of taxodial stupidity resides thereby within, foreunto. And shamefully too I must state. I was desperately trying to get my swollen thing to relax. It was chaffing hard at my denim having stormed its way through the softer white cotton of my Fruit of the Loom briefs. I hate it when these uncontrolled advances advance beyond the protective layers and chaff on denim. It can be very irritating I can tell you. I went into a very philosophical rhetorical oratory about the ignorance of having a tree named for the botanist Douglas as Douglas fir have the Latin name *Pseudotsuga menziesii* after the botanist Menzies.

"It seems after Douglas found it and named it *P. taxifolia* everyone just called it 'Douglas' fir. Then some academic taxonomist found that Menzies had discovered it and it got named *menziesii* because it had priority in time. That is about all I can say about that and you are beyond stunning."

"Keep your eyes on the road please." she demanded in a way that said she really meant it. To the west a great mountain range looked down upon us

I noted the elevation at the summit of Monida Pass as 6870 feet above the sea.

"We are really soaring now. Just look at all those little people so far below us." I said.

"Those mountains over there. It says here they are the Lima Peaks. They are in the Bitterroot Mountains and this is the continental divide. Oh cool, we are in another part of the world. I was going to give her a severe bawling out and discipline her for calling mountains a name like "Lima Peaks" but she preempted me with a question. What is that sign? Stop. I want to see what the sign says?"

The sign informs us that bringing invasive species into Montana is a violation of the laws of Montana and one can be fined 5000 dollars for smuggling invasive species into Montana. I wonder how many people who traverse this pass, enter from the State of Idaho, know what all the invasive species are that are not allowable by the laws of Montana to be brought across this border. I also remembered, not long ago, going the other way where a similar sign informs all persons that it is unlawful to smuggle, or chauffer, or harbor illegal plants, mussels, and other things into Idaho from Montana.

It apparently is not unlawful to transport anything else across the border from or into each of the states as there is no sign prohibiting things like nuclear warheads, illegal immigrants, toxic and explosive matter, prostitutes, molesters, thieves, communists, and I suppose a long list of other things. Now I am in favor of not transporting things that are noxious and that we know become invasive on western rangelands, sagebrush lands, and interfere with croplands.

"The trouble is, it is unlikely more than one in fifty to one hundred thousand who cross this border would recognize more than one or two invasive species." Tanzer pointed out. "Would you, a trained and experienced botanist, know the seeds of crupina, houndstongue, leafy spurge, dalmation toadflax, yellow toadflax, or could you be sure if a sprig of tansy ragwort, Russian knapweed, diffuse knapweed, or perennial pepper weed was hitchhiking on your mud flaps or the radiator grill?
Be honest now Mr. noted Forester and Botanist."

"No."

"No and this illustrates a point I should like to make. Law is an incredibly poor machine at banning stuff, even stuff like noxious weeds, from transport, establishment, and thriving immigrant colonies, just as it is a poor vehicle for banning most other practices and then leaving humans to their own devices. It is even worse when it bans things that should not be banned in the first place."

"Are you an angel?"

"Now why would you ask a stupid thing like that?"

"I just wanted to know. I am not sure sometimes when I am talking to an angel or if it is just a perturbation in my imagination. I have a great imagination you know. It is so good I sometimes cannot tell if it is what is real and the rest of my existence is a fantasy."

We pass by a large blue sign that has a white cross, a Latin cross in its upper left corner. It says "White markers are placed at the location of fatalities in Montana. They are maintained by the American Legion.

I note that white Latin crosses that resemble the instruments used to torture criminals to death in the Roman Empire are here in Montana referred to as white markers. As such they have nothing to do with any notions of an afterlife of any kind. If they did the state might be in violation of crossing a boundary that crossing in America creates great passionate legal debates and interventions.

"You mean like the one where the United States motto that seems to refer to God, does not actually refer to God per the Supreme Court of the United States who said it is a secular motto."

"Precisely, my darling Tanzer. You are most perceptive, I must say."

"I want to see the place you told me about."

"I don't remember telling you about the place I told you about."

"Then just follow the directions I give you. I told you I was a good navigator, so just do what I say. You don't even have to stop at any gas stations and ask either. Besides I want to be sure you see the place and have a firm understanding of it."

I followed her directions and exited the federal highway that I hoped I had helped pay for, drove a gravel road to the west that soon came to public land. A sign said we were driving the Big Sheep Road. Now I felt quite good as I was sure I helped pay for the road. There were towering white limestone formations that soon enough showed up along the road. A nice flowing creek gurgles in the canyon bottom. I assume it is Big Sheep Creek and further reflection says we are in Big Sheep Canyon. The limestone was laid on a carbonate platform of a Mississippian age sea. Then it was warped and tormented deep in the earth and later rose, pushed by the forces that made the Tendoy Range. We drove into what seemed a remoter and remoter valley with immense arching mountains to the west, lots of

Booth's willows, silver hair grass hummocks, cows milling about. We took a detour up a muddy road and saw white primroses growing strangely on the side of hummocks. I was not sure if the woman I picked up days back, that seemed so innocent, was not completely crazy. She seemed crazier than I ever seemed to be myself. And there were times I will tell you I thought I was really crazy. We had to stop and wade through some mud and go look at the primroses. She was overcome with a strange elation. I thought she must be in what I have heard called ecstasy, where one is in some kind of trance, where the woman is in some direct communication with God or something. But I had never seen it. After a long long drink of the sublime beauty of the primroses we withdrew towards the pickup. We were rewarded by a flat tire on the left rear. To my great astonishment the imp with me was true to her word. She had the jack out immediately, the lug bolts off, the truck lifted, and the new tire in place like she was an expert.

"Who taught you to change a tire so well?" I asked.

"Oh it could have been my daddy, or my brother, or a barkeep I once knew."

The father, the brother were just fine with me. The bar guy raised a red flag in front of me. She might have baggage, she might have a beau already, she might not be a virgin, and she might have had an abortion. Holy cow. My mind raced through all these terrible scenes. I was crushed, I think devastated, as a woman once told me about discovering some infidelity in her guy. I was really getting into a funk. I threw the old muddy flat in the bed, got mud in my ear, and hair, and a bunch on my pant's leg. I said nothing. I had to show her I was strong, could throw a muddy tire in the bed of a pickup probably better than she could, by god. I did so, by god, I did. And I went around to the other side of the truck, opened the door for her like a true gentleman as my father had taught me to do in the days before they broke the world, and held out my arm so she could get in. I walked around behind the truck feeling a bit of pride come back in my skull. It was not a huge amount but enough. Not enough to ask about the barkeep and if she was going to marry him when we finished this circumnabulation of the great Yellowstone caldera.

It was some miles further that we stopped. I got out and examined the rocks. There were some piles here and there. Nothing said I could not stop and look at the rocks. There are still a lot of places you can't stop and just look at rocks. People find that very suspicious. But these rocks were the right ones. They have strange lines in them; they are granitic rocks with very strange conical lines in them. They are known as shatter cones.

"Shatter cones can only be made by the most extreme shocks. These were shocked by an extraterrestrial impactor that hit the planet Earth some 900 million years ago," Tanzer the physicist said. "They have survived a shockwave of up to 30 gigapascals. Not many know about them. They occur in various places on the earth where an extraterrestrial immigrant has crashed headlong into our home and given us something to contemplate that is a much greater power than we."

The beauty of Eltanzer in her tight dark brown skirt and muddy boots, and white satin blouse she had somehow donned since I last looked, standing on this rock pile struck me as the only power in the universe I was more impressed with than the tremendous explosion and shock wave that was recorded in these rocks. Eventually we advanced to the north. There was a place I knew of where we could camp and also one I had explored in the past. There were some really cool things I wanted to show her."

We camped in a vacant campground along a small creek. I cooked some ground bison meat I had in the cooler. I added some wild onions from a nearby hill. Made coffee from boiled creek water. It was superb; it was feel really alive time. Spring was thrusting her magnificent resurrection of plants out of their winter hibernation into the full glory of warm days. There were little yellow lilies, bluebells, and globeflowers bursting with energy, busily making new seeds. I was so pulled by the magnetic power to the girl, the Tanzer beam of light, I could hardly stand it. I used every ounce of strength I could muster to stay on my side of the line. Tomorrow I would show her something I was very proud of finding.

Coyotes sang to us sometime during the night. I don't know the melody or the title of their tune but it sounded very deep, probably full of meaning. They were definitely enjoying their concert.

It was chilly in the morning. Took the sun a while to get the day warmed up for business but the chill was great for having morning coffee from my very soot blackened boiler. No filters, no percolator just straight boiled. Pour it in a steel cup, piping hot, sip it, and throw the dregs on the ground. Real cowboy style coffee.

I took her up on this slope where smooth fine grained rocks lay in tiers. These were lacustrine rocks that formed in an ancient lake bed some fifty million years ago, during the end of the Eocene epoch and extending into the Oligocene. There were leaf impressions, twig impressions and the strange fossils of ancient fruits. Here one could see the long history of life on this planet. Here one could see fossils that were like the leaves of trees that now live a long ways away, that are no longer extant in this place. The one I wanted to show her was found in this particular locale. I hit a rock or two with a rock hammer I always carry just for such emergencies as this. It was not long and I found what I was looking for. I held it to the angel.

"Yes, The Secret Society of the Sweet Persimmon is very pleased." she purred.

I knew now there was something about Tanzer that was of immense power. She knew what this was. How could she know this was a fossil of the ancient Persimmon *Diospyros oregoniana* the fruit of a plant now extinct but that is related to the Virginia persimmon *Diospyros virginiana?* The persimmon she knew not long after our first meeting. It was just too improbable.

"How do you know what it is?"

"Hmm. Just guessed at random."

I plowed forward and took her in my arms, held her tight around her sensuous waist, pulled her grand tetons to my breast, and kissed her on the lips. She had, of all things, put lipstick on at some point this morning and I could not get a bearing on just when. It did not matter though. She was a very sensuous, very skilled, completely expert of the first-degree kisser. She kissed back so well it darn near floored me.

"Now, how did you know?" I demanded.

She got this twinkle in her eye and a sassy smile on those magnificent lips, and she must have cast some kind of a spell over me, the kind that only a trained CIA or a KGB agent or a member of the American PSI (The American Persimmon Intelligence Service) which should be the APIS but to throw off other foreign and domestic spy agencies is the APSI. Apis is also the genus name for honeybees so under the rules of priority cannot be used by spy agencies. It really does not matter. What does matter is she had used some kind of advanced psychological mezmerization technology or had surreptitiously injected me with a small dose of brain control enzymes. There really were an endless number of possibilities here.

I told her at this point that I was not for sale. As we drove back along the gravel road I got to thinking this may not have been the smartest thing I had ever told a woman, but it just came out. I saw her laughing about it while more or less turning her head away, pretending to look at roadside flowers, that sort of thing. There was a period of quiet as we drove along the vacant road. We came to a large lake.

"I can feel her," Tanzer whispered.

"Feel who?

The Indian woman. This is where she met her brother when the Lewis and Clark Corps of Discovery came up the Beaverhead River with Clark and Lewis came in from the west with Chief Camehawait. Sacagawea was of the same Shoshoni tribe and had been kidnapped years before.

"You can feel her?"

"I feel her."

I spotted a skein of Canada Geese and some rafting ducks on the big lake.

"Did you know Canada Geese pair bond for life? And so do the mallards in that raft out there. And more than that the female mallard is the dominant decider of the pair," Eltanzer said. "I thought she was a bit proud and a little haughty about this.

"Yes, I replied, but I have seen canvasback and golden eye ducks on this piece of water and they serially monogamous. Each year the females pick a new mate. There are even birds that are polyandrous some simultaneously and some serially like the Phalaropes. Isn't that strange?"

"Maybe you could be serially monogamous. Would you like that?" Eltanzer asked.

That got me wondering. Thinking. Gersh what a tangled web of knots formed in my soul.

We crossed a large earthen dam labeled by humans Clark Canyon Dam. A sign on the right said no stopping on the dam. Another said 45th parallel. Halfway between the equator and the North Pole we were and could not legally stop to enjoy it.

I continued on taking the old frontage road instead of I-15. We passed very pink rocks, conglomerates.

"Nice Cretaceous clasts." She informed me. "And I like the volcano throat standing up ahead. And look at the old Triassic rocks over there. And the Permian up beyond."

I wondered how she knew all this. Not many who drive along this highway even notice, let alone know, what they are looking at. The pages of the history of the earth are written in the rocks but how many stop to read them. Most are going someplace, some destination, and have no time for such learning.

We noticed a profound page in history. Here one can see the Permian Phosphoria formation and on top of it the Triassic Dinwoody. The boundary marked the time when a terrible pall fell over the earth. The oceans were full of sulphate reducing bacteria. The sea life of the Permian largely became extinct. The dawn of the Triassic was born in the death throws of a former age. The continents separated from the single land mass called Pangea. The dark brown chocolate brown of the Dinwoody formation record a big change in the sea floor. If one looks closely here one finds a lot of ancient lampshells called *Lingula*. These are in the phylum that first learned to produce hard shells of calcium carbonate. The have existed from the Cambrian to this day.

"Look up there." she said

A Golden eagle soared way above the old volcano above the columns now called the Organ pipe, columns of dark basalt, millions of years old, Paleogene.

"Oh my. How sad." Tanzer said with a bit of a shocked voice.

"Sad, an eagle makes you sad?"

"This one does. It is seeing over the horizon. It is informing me of a loss. I am afraid we are going to have to pull up for a few days."

"Pull up?"

"Stay a few days. I will try to explain."

I got a room for two at the Paradise Inn in Dillon, Montana. Paradise seemed a good name for a place to stay. I needed to stretch my legs. Too much time in the old pickup saddle without a walk. Should not go so long without a stretch. I walked around the parking lot looking at rocks for a few minutes. When I got to the room Tanzer was sitting on the bed talking on the phone. She had a rather sad look on her pretty face. When she was done she said. "Lets go. I need to move or I'll fall apart".

It was getting dusk as we walked along the UPRR tracks. The tracks were old. They had rolled a lot of heavy steel wheels over the years. Some grain bins showed up. Next ancient brick buildings to the east. A Union Pacific SD 40 Diesel was resting on a siding down the tracks next to a large Union Pacific Emblem on a small grey shack.

"There is someplace right along the tracks I want to show you." Tanzer said.

We came to an old building with a kind of cupola on top. 'Saloon since 1897' was written on the corner door awning. The Metlin Hotel on top. The thing looked pretty old, not so well cared for. We entered. At least I had my own girl with me this time. Would not have to risk talking to or dancing with any strange women. Not as likely to get in trouble as in Wyoming bars. We went to this old wooden bar. She ordered a scotch. I ordered a red wine. I gave up scotch after visiting Scotland and tasting the real thing. They did not have any red wine. I don't drink beer. This was going to be trouble. Ya can't just sit at a bar and not order something. I ordered a Jack Daniels. Took plenty of ice. El Tanzer was very sad. A tear formed in her eye.

"Bad news?" I finally blurted out.

"No not bad news, just sad news. Actually good news for those who are sane. But good news can be sad."

I took a short sip on the Jack Daniels. I noticed Tanzer took just a wee sip herself and was contemplating something. Something was bothering her. Some sad news that was good news.

"Did you know it is a legend around here that Ernest Hemingway came to this bar from time to time, would go fish the Beaverhead, then come here and load up?" she said.

"I didn't know that."

"I thought you would be interested. I know you like to write. Would you like to write like Hemingway?"

"No. Hell no. I would only like to write like me."

"Well, that is a good sign. I have never figured how he could write what he did, *The Old Man and the Sea* for example, and *For Whom the Bell Tolls*, then take his own life over there in Ketchum, Idaho. How could he destroy his own great mind?" she said.

She was brooding on something dark and painful. I wanted to take her in my arms and make it all better. Whatever was bothering her needed to be made all better. It was as if she was experiencing a sadness over Hemingway but that was many years ago.

She said the words of John Donne from which Hemingway took the title.

No man is an island
Entire of itself
Any man's death diminishes me
Because I am involved in mankind,
And therefore never send to know for whom the bell tolls:
It tolls for thee.

John Donne

"It is important we know our ephemeral nature," she said. "But it is hard to embrace it. We want to live forever. And when we see another leave we are so sad. And it hurts. And we try to explain. And we seek solace. We want relief from the horrible pain of loss. And relief is not forth coming."

I walked her back to the room in the man- made light of the small town. There were plenty of neon lights. There were street lights, car lights. There was no longer true darkness of the starry nights of our ancestors. They would have faced death with out any glittering lights. Just the distant stars or the moon.

"We have to wait here until the funeral. I have to say a few words at the funeral; I want you to come with me."

I held her and lay on the bed with her in my arms. I could so easily have lifted her skirt and joined with her in an embrace of pleasure. A brief interlude from the reality of death. But it seemed completely wrong. She did not need that right now. She needed someone who could share the pain of whatever loss she was experiencing. We both drifted into a deep sleep.

In the morning she said, "The interment is not for two days. Let's go out in the prairie today. I want to charge my battery before I must speak."

I drove North old highway 91. At Apex junction the prairie was in bloom with a little yellow plant called Alpine lesquerella. Phlox also spread its little bluish petals all over the place. Blue grama grass turned the prairie green. A strange bird, McCown's longspur, made swoops into the air, then parachuted down in strange twirling decents. We just watched for a while letting the show of plants and birds take over our minds.

"Are you achieving a kenosis?" she asked.

This floored me. It was like a six hundred pound gorilla had just socked me in the jaw. How did she know I needed a kenosis? There it was again that blasted telekinesis that no right minded scientists would say is possible. I had commenced the kenosis before I pulled her out of the river. Actually I did not pull her out of the river. I more or less watched her emerge from the river. It was getting very strange in my mind. I could not sort it out with my reasoning power.

The day wore on. She drove my old battered pickup a while. I don't know how she pulled that off. I am very guarded about who drives my abused machine. But I didn't seem to mind. I did not have to expend any of my mental prowess on driving. I am a very intent driver. When I drive I shut out a lot of things. I even miss a lot of things I would probably like to see. I have even been known to set a peanut butter and pickle sandwich on the passenger seat and ignore it. But I believe in driving so as not to endanger me or any one else. It is just something I do. I really wish a lot of other drivers would do that.

At a little sleepy town named Melrose, Tanzer drove east. We bumped along through rangeland mowed almost clean by cows, along a willow-lined creek. We came to a really odd place. There was a small man- made lake. The road had mud holes in it. Then she stopped and got out. The rocks looked familiar. Yellowish sandstone. I had seen it before. It was the rock that was six thousand feet high on Mt Moran in the Grand Tetons. The flathead sandstone. Cambrian age sandstone. The time when multicellular animals really got going in earnest on this planet. Things like trilobites and brachiopods came to call earth's oceans their home. Flatworms and jellyfish. And corals. There was once an ocean here at this spot in the Northern Rockies. It is a spot where you can see what the geologists call the Great Unconformity. The flathead sandstone of some 550 or so million years rests on ancient basement rocks of Archaean gneiss. Some 2.4 billion years of earth history are missing here. There was no ocean to deposit sediments and the ancient metamorphic rocks were not preserved.

Somehow Tanzer had climbed up a large boulder and gotten to the top of the cliff while I was not paying attention. Seeing her standing up there like she had just grown out of the rock made her look like a Greek sculpture of Pallas Athena or Aphrodite. She was so beautiful. I could see where a skilled Greek sculptor could have gotten his inspiration from. He would have sculpted a goddess of course.

We stayed much of the rest of the day walking over very ancient shales that had trilobite parts in them. Black rocks had white carbonate traces of ancient worm borings. The worms were probably looking for something to eat but here and there the borings of humans in very recent times showed up. They were looking for gold an oddity in the animal kingdom. What other animal would waste his time on such a travesty. Upon completion of our adventure into the ancient Cambrian world we drove back to Dillon for another night in the Paradise. Tanzer was most silent all evening brooding on a mystery she was not yet willing to share with me.

The next day later in the afternoon. I was now driving northeast out of the small town we called home for a brief but eternal time. I was thinking about the old buildings erected in the 1800's as the railroad town it was then. I was thinking on the old Victorian cottages the rail men, the sheep ranchers, the cattle magnates, the bankers, and bartenders built to make use of their new found wealth. I was thinking about one Theophilus B. Craver whose grave we discovered in the morning up on a hill overlooking the town. The symbol of the Grand Army of the Republic was on the granite stone. Before we departed I inquired at the Beaverhead Museum and found the grave was the interment place of a civil war soldier, a soldier who had migrated into the region after the bloodbath that changed our nation in the mid 19th century. He ranched not far from where Tanzer and I discovered the ancient persimmon. The entire place was now devoid of the people who settled these river valleys. It was as if they never existed in the first place except for things like tombstones and brick buildings, many of which were showing signs of age, were crumbling, some abandoned to return to the earth.

I darn near hit a white tailed deer after we crossed the Beaverhead River in a tall *Pragmites* marsh. There were road signs in abundance that warned of need for slowing down. The great Mississippian period limestone Beaverhead Rock stood above the marsh. Here was the rock Sacagawea recalled as the gateway to the country of her people as she waded the river with the Corps of Discovery in 1805. Carrying a baby on her back, she was seventeen or so years old. American History occurred here but it is noted only in occasional road side signs that fewer and fewer are cognizant of. Fewer and fewer can see a beaver in the rocks silhouette. But I can. I knew the beaver well. There were beavers in a place sacred to me in the east. It was highland province lake that was the center of my life in the east. They would come out of their stick house and swim circles around my kayak. They would swim circles around my rowboat when I was casting a bass bug under the birches trying to entice a largemouth bass. They would slap the water with their flat tail and that would be the end of enticing a bass in that vicinity.

"You miss me don't you?"

I did not answer. I was deep in thought. We moved on. Tanzer was unusually silent, brooding on some mystery she did not want to share.

We passed through a small town named after a famous general of the Civil War. It was twilight when we came to an old cemetery. There were graves of children whose lives were snuffed out by scarlet fever or diphtheria. Lives snuffed out before they had a chance at life. The unfairness of it all hit me. Life plays in a world of unfair rules.

The interment was in a small plot at the far side of the cemetery. A long view into the Tobacco Root Range, still snow- mantled, seemed to stare back into the little group assembled. An urn of ashes was in a small opening, dug at the base of a lone pine tree.

The preacher spoke,

"Ashes to ashes, dust to dust"

That was all he said. All he needed to say. Except for a brief introduction.

"Now friends we ask El Tanzer to say a few words written just a few days before."

Tanzer stood beside the small grave. Magnificent and perfect. Awesome and serene. Then she spoke in a soft mesmerizing tone.

Twilight

The twilight comes.
  I hold in mind the flaming circle
Image of the setting sun.
  The twilight comes.

My mind in hope sees sunrise come.
  But knows for me what time has done.
The dawn of peace for me has come
  My twilight time has come

Am I now ready not to see
  The sunrise lighten every tree?

In mornings grand old symphony
The twilight comes.

I sway in anger by my tree.
And plea for time once more to see.
The sunrise on a buzzing bee.
It shall not be,
It shall not be.
The twilight sings its song to me.

With that, I accept what I know must be.

Then El Tanzer went to the open grave and from her breast held a golden oak leaf cluster. For a minute she just beheld the leaves. Some tears fell from her beautiful eyes. She knelt by the grave and placed the oak leaf cluster with the urn.

There was a calm that came over the place. The little clan of friends felt to their core the truth left to them by their friend and read by El Tanzer of the mist. El Tanzer, who I had somehow brought to this place at the right time.

I too felt a profound peace come upon me, I never felt less afraid of death. I was freed from some residual chains that had once bound me. I felt something more when the oak leaf cluster was placed on the urn. I had a sadness for the oak leaf cluster and knew I must understand my grief a little better.

"I will of course help you," Tanzer whispered.

I was again shocked by the knowledge she had of this sadness for the oak leaf cluster. I took her to the shameful wreck I brought her to this place in. I looked all about but no one was left of the funeral attendees. No one was deploring the holy tragic junk heap I called my horse.

We continued our journey, drove through the small Montana towns of Laurin and Alder. Historic Signs told of a world that was once a mad, hell bent for leather, placer gold mining camp. Great semi circular piles of gravel clasts lined Alder Gulch where a great dredge turned the small creek upside down in the gold crazed frenzy of those seeking rapid wealth. There were a few places that said garnets could be found by washing the sands left behind by the gold miners. To my delight cottonwoods and willows grew in abundance, nature unconcerned with the follies of men for acquisition of wealth in golden colors from a stream bed. Very ancient Proterozoic rocks were exposed in the road cut. We passed through the town named for the wife of confederate president Jefferson Davis, Virginia's City. Now a tourist destination, still a functioning county seat, but pretty quiet this early in the spring. The tourist hordes do not arrive till later when schools are out and it is warmer.

There was a sign pointing to the way up to Boot Hill, I thought of driving up to the graves of the hanged road agents of a previous century. Like it would be uplifting. I had already lost the sense of what had just happened. On further reflection I decided this would not be the time to take my companion to the graves of hanged road agents. It suddenly seemed inappropriate. I do not always recognized when something is inappropriate but this time I did. The Tanzer was still brooding. I could tell she was still brooding. She had not even told me who the deceased was. I was clueless as to whether it was a relative, a sister, perhaps a niece. Maybe it was a close friend, a roommate. I did not know and she did not share. So I drove on out of the town named for Jefferson Davis' wife. Up a rather steep hill too I will tell ya. My poor old iron hearted steed did some huffing and puffing, and I was scared a blown head gasket's guts would soon be ornamenting the pavement in an oily slick of disaster. I went real slow. I am good at communicating with machines so they don't just collapse in smoke and oil slicks. Always have been. I can almost always get the most out of a lawn mower, a hay swather, a tractor, a chain saw. You name it. If it has gears I can get the most out of it.

I got the poor old bastard to the summit, went over the high point and pulled into an overlook to give the obviously out of breath engine a break. Before us the great Madison Range rose over the river valley. This is the same Madison River that emerges from the Yellowstone where the Firehole and the Gibbon merge at Madison Junction right at the Caldera rim of the last eruption of the dysphoric sleeping giant.

Eltanzer got out of the truck, put her hand to cover her eyes, and took in the great view of the range.

"I want to go in there. For a while. Can we go in there for a while?" she said pointing to a high peak.

I should have known the name of it but of course because I am against naming peaks in the first place I did not know it. I once lived on the other side of it and am pretty sure I knew its name. That was probably before I learned the names of peaks is nothing more than mind clutter. This mental trash does nothing but fill the available neurons with useless information that only inhibits important things. Important things such as thinking about how mountains came about in the first place. The earth was once a big liquid ball of iron surrounded by magmatic stuff. According to astrophysicists, who are smarted than I am, the iron core got surrounded by mineral conglomerations of rocky stuff called the Mantle and then an outer solid rock layer called the crust developed. We learned that in high school, at least those of us who stayed awake part of the time, and took a break from trying to look up girls dresses without being noticed. Since no one has ever succeeded in traveling to the core or the mantle this is largely information derived from indirect means like the patterns of seismic waves. In my opinion this is not greatly different than learning about girls either. Indirect means are generally required. Learning to figure things out from indirect methods is helpful fore those who want to explore what the meaning of existence is. It is akin to getting to the hot liquid charged ball of iron. If you ever get there you're a fried chicken.

For some very odd reason I leaned on the truck and wondered what would happen if it was crumpled into a nice ball of iron by a large very powerful hand, and the hand took it up into the clouds and dropped it and it commenced falling towards the earth at 32 feet per second per second as I once learned in college physics where I paid a little more attention to the professors since I was a complete failure by this time at looking up girls skirts in class. I just never got good at it without being caught and embarrassed so I more or less stopped trying. By the way, our society and its protocols have changed and this practice is no longer considered a benign expression of adolescent curiosity. It is on the list of inappropriate and even illegal actions. So I no longer recommend it. I return to wondering what happens if the ball keeps on falling, plows through the crust, the mantle, accelerating at thirty-two feet per second per second and reaches the core. What happens when it gets right to the center? Stop suddenly? Keep going until it shoots out the other side of the earth and off into space.?

Tanzer was giving me this look of desperation. Holy frogeyes. She was beautiful, magnetic, and vulnerable. It took care of the gravity and the iron ball problem for the time being.

"Of course we can go up there. We can stay as long as we want." I said.

I don't remember for sure how long we were in those mountains. We walked mostly off trails in what appeared to be a wilderness. We slept under the stars. One night I saw in the very clear sky a faint constellation that hardly anyone sees any more. The sky is so full of haze and soot from our economic pursuits you can't see faint stars so much. This one got there by a rather strange way. It seems an ancient king named Ptolemy of Alexandria went off to war to avenge the murder of his sister. It must have been a fairly risky war as to whether he would succeed and return. But he had a wife who must have thought a good deal of him. So she did what was the scientific and best thing in those days; she went to the goddess Aphrodite's Temple and implored the goddess to bring her husband home safely. To seal the deal, Berenice (that was the king's wife's name) promised the great goddess she would cut her beautiful tresses of hair and give them to the love goddess who must have been very much into this kind of thing. Ptolemy won, came home safely, and Berenice cut her hair and put it in the temple. Aphrodite was so pleased she took the hair and placed it among the constellations of the starry night. We were looking at it as the constellation, Coma Berenices.

"It is still there," Tanzer whispered.

The next morning after the sun had been up a while and there was a little warmth we came upon a clump of purple blossoms that were so stunning we could do nothing but pause and visit them a while.

"Pasque flowers," she said.

"What does pasque mean? Do you know?" I asked.

"It is French. It means associated with Easter. The Pasque flowers emerge from the ground as if they were dead, and resurrected. A kind of metaphor for the belief in the resurrection of the dead."

"Do you believe in resurrection from full death?"

"To me it is a psychological way to avoid the reality that we are physical beings with an ephemeral time on this planet, that ends and we swim in an eternal unconscious peace. We return to the ashes or to the dust. Our molecules, and elements are used again but never again do we live, have friends, laugh, play, drink red wine, and make love as the person we were during our brief sojourn in time. So many ideas to the contrary emerged in the ancient minds of the Egyptians, the Mesopotamians, and in the bronze aged city of Ugarit. The Greek pantheon was full of gods and goddesses who intervened in human affairs. Some like the fates directed the destiny of men and women right down to the time and manner of death. These mystical beings and their powers were transcribed and evolved as authority since they came from ancestral times. And humans revere ancestral wisdom and find it almost impossible to let go.

"So you do not believe we continue in some conscious state after death?"

Before I could answer, suddenly she hit me between the eyes with:

"I want to make love with you. I want to fill this time with happiness and pleasure. I want to join with you in eternity which is right now. You are the one I choose. I choose you of my own free will because my heart chooses you."

I was in some rather strange place. I normally don't make love to just anyone. I might think it a good thing to do but I made that doggone promise to me that I would not do the full on sexual union with a woman just for the pleasure of a few minutes. I wanted someday to have a wife. I wanted the kind of wife like King Ptolemy had in Queen Berenice who would give up her glory for him. And I wanted to be able to say to the woman I was pure virgin for her. I wanted to promise to be faithful to her. And now here I was in the thrall of this gorgeous, beautiful, Tanzer who was offering me what practically every man on this planet spends countless hours convincing himself is what should be his right as a man. To have beautiful, sex crazed females demand he have unbridled sex with them.

"What a mess, I have not cleared up the iron ball problem and now you want to make love?" was all I could come up with.

She broke into a big grin. She came over and put her arms around my neck and gave me a very big kiss squarely and expertly placed. Delicious, utterly and excruciatingly delicious.

"What iron ball problem?" she asked. "Are you having iron ball problems?"

I hated even thinking about iron ball problems right now.

"I just can't right now, blast it Tanzer darling. I want to. Don't get me wrong, I don't know if I can not do it. It may be you will have to stop me from doing anything more than just kissing you. I don't even know for sure who you are. You have not even told me who we interred."

"I will tell you sometime. Just not right now. Please, ok?"

"Ok. I think we need to go out of the mountains for a while. We are getting a little low on food. I am getting tired of digging up bulbs, and scraping the inner bark of trees, and and."

"Hmm. The mountain men would not have taken such an attitude."

"Those were different times, and they did go into the valleys and trade, and they hunted without any thought of whether it was hunting season, and they took wives or traded for wives, and their wives knew how to preserve berries, and cook. Darn, it was just different times."

All at once it clouded up. A brisk wind swayed the spruce and fir violently, the sky darkened. Thunder rolled through the great mountain range shaking it seemed even the bedrocks. We hunkered next to a big crack in the granite. Suddenly as a lightening bolt ripped the heavens apart followed by a terrible crash of angry waves I was transported through a time machine of sorts. I was very young. The sky had darkened over the granite hills surrounding my lake. Lightening had flashed. I was sitting in a boat with a poncho casting a worm hoping for a crappie to strike just off this large granite protuberance jutting into the lake. Many stumps of long felled trees often harbored crappies. Quickly I donned an old battered poncho, grabbed the oars of this old wooden rowboat and tugged with all my strength. Large droplets pelted the lake making big rings and went poof poof on my poncho. I gained the shore as a new blast of anger from the sky flashed and growled. I pulled the boat into wet bushes and move away from the shore. Overhead a great roar emanated from the canopy of oaks and hickories. It did not last long until the rain became more of a steady drizzle, the canopy roar a gentile murmur. The T storm was just on the front of a larger system that would soak the forest for at least a day. Often these days interrupted a great summer month with soaking wet dismal sogginess. I suddenly was transported back to the Madison Range. Days where it rained in the arid west were now treasured by my psyche. Where they once interrupted a good days fishing now they were a welcome reprieve from the constant dryness of the arid west. I wished the storm would have stayed and made it wet and soggy and dismal for a while. But it did not last.

"You miss those big raindrops on a highland lake and the murmur from the oak canopy don't you?"

I gave Tanzer a grumpy look. I did not want to give her the satisfaction of an answer like I was heartsick over missing an eastern drizzle. I just did not want to show that kind of weakness. No sir, I did not want to give even a tiny whimper of such a weakness. It would be considered unmanly is all I can say about it. If you are un-manly in the western mountains you are doomed. A grizzly bear will notice you are un-manly and you may get taught a good mauling lesson. I have heard of such things happening. It suddenly came to my attention that the Griz inhabited the very mountain range we had been submersed in. I checked my belt and to my great relief discovered I had not forgotten to fasten two canisters of pepper spray. Maybe I was not as negligent as I thought I was although I don't recall putting the bear spray on in the first place. I must have trained myself to do this automatically, subconsciously. It was a lot like taking a poncho with you on a fishing foray on an eastern lake. Of course you only need one poncho. But in Griz country you need two pepper sprays, and two extra in your pack. I would have you take three pepper sprays if you had three hands. But two hands are all most of us have. Why? What if ya have a territorial dispute with two bears at the same time? What if one canister fails to spray? What if a Grizzly bear and a giant behemoth decide to maul you at the same time?

"Ok, that is enough." Tanzer growled. "We are out of here before any big things have to be dealt with."

We left the mountains that day. I am not sure how long we were in them either. I did not look once at my watch or mark the sunrises on my pistol handle. I was real glad when we got back to the old iron horse. I had stashed some mixed nuts and dried berries, and was glad we had the ability to move stuff like that better than the mountain men would have been able to do. There are always some things that are worse than they were in the past and some things are the same as they were in the past and some things are better.

"This is one of the things that is better than the mountain men had," I proudly informed the impish one.

"What is better?"

"This. These canned nuts and a can of sardines. Some dried raspberries. You want some? It is probably better than those poor pelt collectors had in the mountain man days. These nuts came from all over the place, Brazil, California, the southern pacific. The sardines from the Pacific but who knows where. It is the enormous economic machine that drives so many of us mad that put these vittles in our reach here in the cold Northern Rockies where none of them are grown."

I stopped at this little known hot spring on my way to the halfway point of this circumnabulation thing I embarked on. I am still not sure why I embarked on it other than to impress "Starlight" whoever she was. This spring had a sign on it that God soaked in the hot spring or maybe it was the "Waters of the Gods, it could have been Norris' hot tub." I don't really remember. I will say Tanzer warmed up the place in this two piece bathing suit she scrubbed up. I was doing everything possible to keep from embarrassing myself in front of this couple of not so good looking, not so prim, actually rather obese women who were also soaking in the divine tub. It felt good I will say. I was a little achy after several years in the wilderness. It wasn't really several years but it seemed like it. All at once it hit me. The solution as to why the iron ball falling at thirty two feet per second per second does pass through the center of the earth. It was that blasted Newton, Isaac Newton Sir that figured it out. Of course he went a little nuts when an apple bonked him and woke up some sleeping neurons.

$$F = (G) \frac{mass\ 1\ X\ mass2}{D\ squared}$$

So there it was. A solution. As the ball gets to the center the denominator approaches Planks distance and becomes zero and there is no longer any force. But the iron ball is still in motion. So when the iron ball gets to the center it just keeps on going. It keeps going until it gets way back towards the surface under the Indian Ocean. Then the mass of the earth that has now become rather large in comparison to the ball slows the ball until it stops and recommences a journey to the center again. This is just a thought experiment where reality can be dismissed during the thought.

"Just what is Plank's distance?" Tanzer asked.

"Plank's distance is so short that nothing can be shorter. It is on the order of 1.616,199 X 10 to the minus thirty five meters. It takes light 10 to the minus forty three seconds to traverse it."

"Why just do a thought experiment. Why not a real one?"

"It has something to do with the earth becoming very hot and then the rocks becoming viscous, then liquid, then I suppose liquid iron. Boring a hole through liquid rock and iron to drop the iron ball through is problematical. The stupid ball would also melt."

"So no one will ever know the truth about the ball. Right? No one will ever be able to do the experiment. Right?"

Tanzer was just laid back enjoying the gift of the gods from the ground and did not seem as interested in this as she was in Berenices' hair and how it got in the night sky. Women seem to me to like more emotional content in their explanations than math is capable of putting forth.

When I was finished and had added the formula for calculating the volume of a sphere that came into my mind and I thought was truly very beautiful, as I lay there in the hot divine water my water sprite lifted up these dark sun glasses she came up with. With eyes sparkling like the morning dew in late summer she said, "I want to make love to you, Mr. Newton. It is really quite simple. You do not by the way need a formula and it is even more beautiful than the volume of sphere."

I wished the two rather matronly patrons with us that day had not heard Tanzerita say that, but they did. One however, I must admit, seemed to think it was funny. She flashed eyes at me and more or less bit her lip. I got the message.

Now it turned out we got our aches soothed, our skin wrinkly, enough soaking in holy water, and were driving east again when we came to the last and only undamed river in the State of Montana. Black Cottonwoods grew all long its banks and some had toppled into the gravel having had their roots undercut by a wild flowing river. I got out and waded a minute in the clear cold water. Just to feel one of the sources of the Missouri in its still wild headwaters state. The Gallatin River still flowed free. I took Tanzer by the hand and led her to the gurgling eddies. She was of course right at home, waded into the flowing waters as easily as she had emerged from the Snake to come into my life for this thing I was on.

She asked me as the water swirled around our knees, "Are you getting less angry over the things that mean absolutely nothing?" Things like raging at the mountains with names on them. Names given by men to what seem eternal monuments, but will someday be washed, clast by clast, sand grain by sand grain, into the sea just like the pebbles we are standing on now."

"When you put it that way, my lovely darling, Tanz, I see your point."

"And of course as the ancient Greek Heraclitus, said, 'You can never step in the same river twice.' Just look at the cold flow about us and see that truth. So, I want you to stop raging about things that will not last and spend more time in the spell of the great, but not eternal hills."

We soon enough re-entered civilization. Housing tracts were all over the place. Large gasoline plazas resided at busy intersection. Stores showed up as did auto sales lots with nothing under $20,000 worth buying. The houses seemed excessive, too many garage doors, too many floors, huge windows, expensive trim, paved driveways. We passed furniture stores, malls. The population of Bozeman, Montana had burgeoned since I once lived here. It sprawled all over the Gallatin River Valley. It was now an expensive town. I wondered where all the inhabitants here managed to make enough money to live in this way. There seemed no longer an agricultural base of great significance, no sawmills, just an oil burning horde of vehicles.

"You know I seem to remember seeing a news broadcast not too long ago that said more Americans think the country is on the wrong track." El Tanzer said as she took in the machine that people now live in.

"Ya, hardly any one remembers when communities were for people, when production was done by small businesses of craftsmen, or even large corporations who hired craftsmen and paid them well. Now it is a scramble to make even enough to rent a one room apartment while servicing wealth that can afford these houses, these high tech cars, trucks, and buy stuff in barrels from these malls. So more and more see the wealth owned by fewer and fewer and they can't get there. They can't find happiness in an old nineteen fifties pick-up truck, and time in the Mountains. They can no longer feel pure wondrous joy in touching their feet into the wild upper Missouri headwaters. They no longer even know the history of a place or seem to care. Their relationships, the ones that count, like between lovers, are now torn to shreds by the great invisible hand that requires them to desire the goods we see here. It is as if here is everywhere in America. So the pollsters ask 'are we on the right track or the wrong track?' More and more, in huge numbers, the answer they get is 'we are on the wrong track.' You can be on the wrong track because you wanted to go from Chicago to Seattle but got on the train to Houston. The tracks are well taken care of, the signals working, and the sleeper up to snuff. But when you get off in Houston you stamp your feet and say 'God damn it! I was on the wrong track.' Another case is simply you got on the train to Seattle just fine. The dining car was in operation just fine, had delicious cusine, great red wine. But the signals were not working so well due to low paid workers not giving that much of a damn, and the tracks were just barely holding up. Even though your train was going at a slower than possible rate of speed it was too late when your engineer, who had not gotten enough sleep and his wife had screamed at him that she would never let him touch her again and was leaving with the kids, saw the high balling coal train coming at him from around a bend. The high ball was carrying a hundred coal cars on their way to the Powder Basin for refills, refills to ship coal to China to make the stuff the invisible hand demands we buy. It was too bad so many lost their lives in that train wreck. You survived with a ruptured spleen, three fractured ribs, pins in both tibias, and loss of sight in one eye. You were lucky and you had health insurance but to this day you believe the whole country is on the wrong track."

"That was a long speech. But needed I suppose. Maybe you should run for office, do something to fix the signals, or even better yet lay two tracks."

"Humans could find a way to screw up ten tracks unless their attitude changes. Money must again serve people, but I do not know how to do that except for one thing. And I can not do that, not from elected office, not from the Whitehouse or the Senate, not from the Supreme Court or the head of a major corporation. So I drive around in this old wreck trying to just be happy without stuff."

Suddenly a thought came into my mind. Americans including me are a shifting lot. We rarely live in one place for a lifetime. Even if we grow up in one town, one place, upon graduation from high school is but a mandatory ticket to leave the place we knew as home. And I thought maybe no longer being a part of the place you were born, were a natural part of, creates a festering wound in our psyche. We try to heal or cover up that hole with a quest for adventure or to find a new home and to fill our lives with stuff, but never does stuff heal that loss of no longer belonging to a place that was by birth our natural home. Before I reached any resolution of this strange hypothesis I was interrupted by my companion.

"Let's stay in an old dilapidated dump tonight." Tanzer purred blowing a little tweet in my ear. "One of those run down dumps that still survive from the forties or something, where the water does not work right, and the floors stink, and the chairs stink like stale smoke, and the air conditioner is broken. Kind of like the places described in *Lolita*, you know, what was his name "Humperniclkle" or the likes."

"You totally slay me, Miss Tanzer. One minute you are the smartest woman I ever met, next you play dumb. It was 'Humbert Humbert' not 'Humpernickle' and the literary art of *Lolita* is spectacular, encompassing a story line that is intolerable. I suppose if it had been written anywhere but here with our first amendment freedom of speech and all, it would not have been necessary to publish it in another country well before it could be smuggled back here and published. We are not always entirely sane in my opinion. There are times when I am convinced we are mostly insane."

"There, over there is a dump."

Later after becoming usufructs of room 22 for at least a night, the great light that had entered my life from the Snake River and I discovered a patch of weeds growing in the vacant lot behind the dump. The patch of weeds was alive with a history lesson. At least for those who have studied history.

"Those are Themistocles skippers," El Tanzer informed me.

"They are indeed," I replied. She seemed to be returning more to her self, noticing things like little butterflies happily nectaring on weeds on a vacant lot waiting for a bulldozer to raze it, to put up another bank or something. "Those are *Polites themistocles*. They are named after one politician who got it right on the order of two thousand five hundred years ago. And hardly an American knows his name. Themistocles lived in Athens and was also a visionary and a general. Against the majority he advocated building a Navy. It was not easy to get the wealth loving Athenians to build a navy and they did not give Themistocles all the ships he thought needed. But they gave him some. It was not long and the Persians invaded Greece. The Greeks lost the Battle of Marathon that we still celebrate today with marathon races all over the country. It was not looking good for the Greeks until Themistocles, using his much smaller but better commanded Navy, set a trap in the Straights of Salamis. Themistocles won the battle that many consider one of the most significant history changing fights. He saved Hellenistic culture that still so strongly influence the world today. Maybe he even saved Aphrodite and then later Berenice's and her hair and all that stuff so we could see Coma Berenice's hair in the wilderness. And here he is, remembered by only those few in America who still savor the magnificence of a little Lepidoptera named after a great Greek general who hardly any one in America ever heard of.

"You want me to be your Lolita tonight?" Tanzer the moonbeam purred.

"No Tanzerita. I want to be sane, I want you to be Tanzer, not some, not some,... I forgot what I don't want you to be. You have this affect on me or is it effect? I don't know which. I am getting all wound up again. I wish you would not get me all wound up like that all the time."

"That looks like some prostitutes going in that bar door over there. Do you want me to go hire one for you so you can unwind this evening? I could go walk about uptown a while. Maybe buy some stuff."

"How do you know they are prostitutes?" I asked my sweet, innocent, bright eyed, water nymph from the Snake River.

"You can tell by their clothes, the length of their skirt, the color combination of their outfits, the heels, the make-up. Every ordinary male knows what a prostitute looks like by the way she dresses. My Gosh, you are being naïve with me. Of course you may not be so ordinary. You might be unrepentantly un-ordinary. Again you want me to go hire one for you?" Tanzer the siren blasted in my ear.

I just almost lost it right then and there. I did give her a reasonable loving pat on her very shapely, attractive feminine rear. She more or less flashed her eyes at me that said thank you for your appreciation but you are not supposed to do that these more enlightened days. It was likely not something I would spend the night in jail about for assault and battery even though technically it met all the legal specifications for assault and battery. I thought it was a piece of good luck no sergeant deputies and the like observed the whole thing and the specifications written up and I would have to explain to a judge why it was not what was clearly the case. It would be hard to explain to a judge also about the whole context, the skippers, Themistocles, my loss of mental function over imagining a couple of hussies entering a bar door in high heels, lipstick smeared on their face, skirts of the kind professionals in their profession don, according to my encyclopedically versed Tanzer, to go hunting. I would describe them further but if you don't know what they looked like I suspect you are not old enough or at least mature enough or knowledgeable enough to be reading this book. So I won't give such a graphic account.

Eltanzer realizing I needed some time alone strode off towards the old downtown. I watched her confidently striding the sidewalk. Strangely she was suddenly wearing a pony tail that bounced back and forth. I did not remember her having a pony tail earlier in the day and wondered how she managed to make such an interesting coiffure without my noticing.

I went in the room and picked up a newspaper that had a story on page two about the decline of the sage grouse and attempts by the government to do something about it. The bird might be listed under the Endangered Species Act of 1973. I read of the enormous decline in sage grouse population numbers from millions to only about half a million, maybe less. This decline occurred through a large portion of the northwestern United States. Such things as habitat loss, habitat fragmentation, oil and gas development, were cited as causal. I wondered if we know much about causation of population crashes. There were, if I recollected correctly, estimates that as many as 500,000,000 species that have arisen in the 3.8 billion years since life has been first detected on this planet. Now it is estimated there are about 30,000,000 species. Of course for the majority of the time the modal organisms were the Archea and the Eubacteria. I got to thinking again as frequently occurs when I read this kind of article about what a species is. The old notion of there being defined species that are immutable, as described by old Carolus Linnaeus in his works including <u>Species Plantorum</u> for plants and <u>Systemae Natura</u> for animals has vexed scientists ever since. Trying to make an organism fit into the Kingdom Plantae or the Kingdom Animalia was still an academic goal when I was in high school biology and even unto college biology. First proposed by Aristotle, that idea remained firmly embedded in the human consciousness, even the scientific consciousness, until very recent times. Now I think most biological scientists were very skeptical of the idea that bacteria were primitive plants as it stated in one of my biology books. They figured out that the bacteria were prokaryotes and the animals and plants were eukaryotes and that this was one of the sharpest delineations in the classification of organisms out there in nature. They knew of course that the belief that plants were created on the third day, as proclaimed in the book of Genesis and believed by literalists, was not supported by the book of nature that showed land plants to be the last of the organisms to arise. It was not until the Silurian Period that these amazing beings show up. While animals show up in the time frame of 600 million years ago they do not become abundant in the book of nature until the Cambrian Period about 540 million years ago.

I again stopped here and wondered about what was wondering about the nature of organisms. What is the mysterious thing called consciousness that even makes me aware of there being a problem to solve such as what is a species. I got sort of lost in this whole fantasy. I knew because scientists such as Carl Woese at the University of Illinois during the 1980s had discovered the difference between the Archea and the common bacteria. Primitive plants were thought to be in the same Kingdom as bacteria when I was born some forty years earlier. This was a profound misunderstanding of the nature of life at the time. It has also been discovered now that what was called a species of plant or a species of animal is really a consortium of eukaryotic and prokaryotic cells. Take the prokaryotic cells out of a plant and the plant no longer performs photosynthesis in its chloroplasts that are really cyanobacteria like organisms. Take the prokaryotic cells out of a human gut and the eukaryotic cells that are left can't feed themselves. So what is a species other than a consortium of both prokaryotic and eukaryotic cells working in concert.

I wondered what was declining in the thing they called sage grouse. Was it the eukaryotic cells or the prokaryotic cells? Then I went off on another tangent. We had driven through and about the sagebrush for the past several weeks. The sagebrush was the habitat of the declining descendant of the dinosaurs. I was thinking of the bugs and that I did not notice as many splattered on my windshield as I used to. I got to thinking about a bug I used to hear about from my old college advisor. It was called the rangeland grasshopper. Its scientific name is *Arphia conspersa*. Of course locusts were among the scourges used by God as reported in the Book of Exodus. Since then grasshoppers have been on the human crap list. To the ordinary person, lumping all grasshoppers into one group and putting all on the crap list is just a normal thing to do. Migratory grasshoppers that sometimes swarm over the land devouring the wheat, barley, corn and screen doors of dry land farms have been the target of massive chemical and biological warfare for centuries. In many dry land farming operations they are still a vexation. But one of the great locust populations famous in stories of the previous century has become extinct. The migratory grasshopper *Melanoplus spretus* is no longer among the denizens of the planet. Except as frozen bodies in a few disappearing glaciers of the mountain west. Many would, under the lumping principle, just say "great!"

So it is clear in this fantasy world I am now in that rangeland denizens can and do rather rapidly become extinct. I wonder at this junction if it is the insects that are plummeting in populations all over the United States that are the weak link in Sage Grouse. I get out my computer, hook up to the internet, and commence a little electronic research. It is not long that I find that sage grouse chicks are totally dependent on a diet of insects for about the first three weeks of their life. Then they shift to eating sagebrush. Here I recall a strange thing about the rangeland grasshoppers. They over winter as fifth instars hidden in the grass and duff of their rangeland homes. They could be one of the ready sources of insect gruel for sage grouse chicks. But nothing is ever so simple. There is almost never a simple answer to nature like that. The sage chicks also feed on other bugs including ants and beetles. Still I cannot shake off a gut feeling that the reported declines in bees, wasps, butterflies, sexton beetles, skippers, and many others is a yellow flag staring us in the face. When a yellow flag is waved at high speed drivers in our great passion for high speed dangers at racetracks, the signal means slow down, hold position, there is a dangerous situation ahead.

That is what we need to focus on here I believe. The real world of making money could care less about grasshoppers and sage grouse. Grasshoppers? They are still thought of as pestilences and therefore expendable and despised. Sage grouse? Just collateral damage. But just as we have learned that species are not fixed and immutable organisms but rather consortiums so are ecosystems consortiums. And insects do things in that consortium we are just now beginning to understand. And many of us think sage grouse are awesome. Perhaps before we let them go extinct we can learn something about our own prospects for survival.

I shift to wondering if we have any seers of the nature of Themistocles who may be able to get our recalcitrant money makers to fund a navy that in the future will change history. Or will we fail to heed our Themistocles and become part of the fossil record much sooner than our young consortium of prokaryotes and eukaryotes might attain. There is no law I am aware of that says a big brain and the prized intelligence we hold out as our greatest contribution to the universe has any survival advantage in the face of the billions of years of life on the earth. It could just as easily be snuffed out by an asteroidal impact or a volcanic eruption spewing enormous quantities of sulphur dioxide into the atmosphere changing it from an oxidizing one to a reducing mix of gases. Those are both in evidence as events in the history of our planet.

Our numbers have sky rocketed in this century. Some believe those numbers are enough with our burning of fossil fuels to alter the atmosphere to our detriment. We seem quite well enough able to change our habitat to accommodate to temperature variations. We can survive in cold and hot so long as food is available. But if a volcanic eruption spews great quantities of dust into the stratosphere, blocking sunlight for even as little as a few years, then land plants will fail to produce enough food. With the oceans being exploited as heavily as they have been over the last hundred years there is unlikely to be a back up in the waters.

I woke up from this place I went to in my consciousness. It was a thought experiment I realize. During my adventure into thought the gorgeous Tanzer had returned. I had not noticed her return nor that she donned a bathrobe and is combing her hair. She has apparently just taken a shower.

"I took a shower. After I got back from a wonderful stroll I noticed you were staring blankly at the wall. I was a little concerned to be perfectly honest with you. I thought maybe you had a stroke or something. I even checked your pulse and it seemed normal and your breathing was normal. But you seemed in some deep thought. So I decided you were on one of your mental excursions. So I took a shower."

"Where did you go?"

"I went to town and walked about old town Bozeman. The question is where did you go?"

"I don't know. I just get to thinking about stuff. I am annoyed I can not come up with anything worth testing. I just keep doing thought experiments that are largely untestable. It is very frustrating Tanz. It is very frustrating. Trying to figure out a way to do an experiment that controls thousands and thousands of variables and come up with a little advance in human knowledge. Ya know it amazes me how few seminal thinkers have ever been able to design such experiments either. Like Einstein and Darwin. They mainly observed the universe, wondered about what light was, or watched bugs, and dogs and then they went someplace in their minds. They saw stuff in their minds they could not prove. They could never figure out the practical ways to show their ideas were true. No. It took a lot of other people to make measurements. So far general relativity holds as at least partially the way the universe is. The velocity of light is the only known constant at 186, 282 miles per second. And natural selection remains as the way organisms change over time. Some invisible hand determines who is adapted to some little niche. Over eons of time its genetic compliment pairs of thymine and adenine and guanine and cytosine direct its basic structure and means of making a living. As long as it can make a living in its little piece of the universe it survives. If it can't it leaves no descendants and becomes extinct. If it is a eukaryote its bacterial consorts help with the structure and battle with the world. Those little workers make the organism its building materials and supply it with energy."

"You think about this when you go away for a while?"

"Yes, and just now it floats into my brain something else. It is **The Splatter Hypothesis**. Shit! I need a piece of paper."

"The what hypothesis?"

"Splatter Hypothesis."

"And that is?"

"Simple. When I was younger and through much of my life it seemed whenever I rode in a car, or drove a car in the summer months the windshield got splattered with bugs. Lots of bugs. Now for the last several years it seems I can drive a lot longer without having to clean the bug guts off my windshield."

"And the hypothesis?"

"Flying bugs are attracted to carbon dioxide. We have built enough vehicles of all kinds that create these long tubes of carbon dioxide covering our high speed highways that there have been enough bugs attracted to the high speed windshields to reduce many bug populations. Add the devastation brought about by insecticides and a lot of habitat loss to urbanization and presto, flying bug populations plummet. Along with them bug feeding birds, bats, and other animals and a spiral of declines in the biosphere results."

"That seems logical, even possible. Why don't you write it up?"

Because there are too many variables to control, and it would cost way too much, and I don't even know what kind of experiment to do to test the whole squirming mess. It galls me it does. It galls me."

"Stop. I have had enough academics for this evening. Come with me, in here now. I want to make yowie with you."

"Yowie, how do you know about yowie? You are scaring me, Miss Tanzer, How do you know? I dare you to tell me how you know."

"You know very good and well how I know. I don't do dares either. I am Tanzer not an odds maker. I dare say I do not do dares. Ok?"

"Of course if you say so. Of course it is ok. I am, I am very, I don't know what I am very. I must be insane, I am extremely fig Newton. I am very tired, I am overly aroused about something I cannot grasp, I don't understand what is happening now. It is going on someplace in my sphere, I mean my globe, not exactly, what I am trying to say is…. My god what are you doing?"

"You know what I am doing so stop fussing. I have had about enough fussing for the evening. After all that stuff about the velocity of light and bug hypotheses.

I awoke in the morning. Her majesty was still sleeping in the bed. She had on a black brassiere that had a snap on the back. I wondered what would happen if I undid it. I was certainly interested in having a look at those grand tetons she sported. But I decided it might be better to get up, do the normal stuff one does when they get up; that is, shake off the sleepiness, douse face in basin, take a superb pee, make a lot of chugging kind of racket with the stream, make bubbles if possible. The morning pee is so full of stuff worked over in the nephrons, determined of no further use and out it goes into the pee. Floss teeth, fart, swish teeth, and shower, dry off, comb hair, shave, and get a cup of coffee.

Tanzer woke up while I was peeing. Some women don't mind but I was hoping she would stay asleep. Peeing well requires concentration and I don't like being disturbed. I don't like any of the old residual embarrassment that sometimes occurs when you are peeing in earshot of a woman. Some women still consider peeing an uncouth matter. Or at least something that should be kept secret. Oh, they know you have to do it but they don't want to know you do it. If they are a woman and you're a man that is. They are not nearly so fussy with other women. At least that is what I have been told. I can't verify this from personal experience as I am not a woman. Oddly however, Tanzer did not seem to be like other women in this regard. She just called when I sort of shut the stream down when I realized she was awake and could hear and said, "Get that started again. It is not good physiology to stop like that in mid stream. Besides I am going to check a few things when you are done showering and it would be best if you don't have to go pee and interrupt."

I spent the whole time in the shower worried about what was going to be checked when I got out. Tanzer came in while I was in the shower and went herself with apparently no embarrassment or trepidation. This muse really had me in a strange state of mind. She was an ideal mystery to me. I could not solve her at all. I spent a lot of time drying off trying to figure out how to handle this crisis. Eventually I got dressed and came out. There was Tanzer just prime and beautiful as could be sitting on the chair with her legs crossed and a cup of coffee in her hand and one waiting for me.

"You sure took long enough. Did you save some hot water for me?"

"Yes, plenty."

I was quite relieved that she was not going to do some kind of scrotum check or maybe a prostrate exam as I had been utterly paranoid about after she said she was going to check something and that it was better if I had finished going pee to do. The way things were going you never knew what this magnetic attractor was capable of or would do and I would have no way to defend myself. That is if she wanted to cast one of her mind spells over me, the kind I was sure had happened last night. Try as I might I could not remember what happened last night. For all I knew she could have done just about anything she wanted. She could have said this is something that arouses me but it is not mainstream. Still I want to do it. I want to do it tonight, I want to do it with you tonight because I have chosen you as my man and you must obey. I took a sip of the hot coffee. It was utterly delicious, cooked just right, the way I like it. Tanzer knew just how to do this. She knew everything. I was amazed, excited, aroused, interested, and hopelessly in love with my river sprite.

To my great surprise when she had finished her shower, and female chores, the ones I will not describe here because I don't know a damn thing about them and it would not be prudent anyway. When she got done she wanted to find a good place to have breakfast. One she said that did not have a lot of campfire charcoal, and bits of insects, and leaves in it. So we checked out of the motel and went driving around until I spotted a place to get some breakfast food that was not too unhealthy. It is very hard these days to find a restaurant that serves mostly healthy food for breakfast. For example most places think everyone wants eggs, bacon, toast, hash browns, pancakes made with wheat flour, donuts, and orange juice. Once in a while you can substitute apple juice or cranberry. No American restaurant has such things as almond flour pancakes or free range eggs where the chickens graze on green pasture, catch insects, and avoid heavy doses of grain jammed down their gullets. Perhaps some grass fed bison or beef strips for the meat adherents. Nothing with a load of nitrites, sulphites, and insecticides in it. No transfats, hydrogenated oils, or massive doses of refined sugar masqueraded as donuts, French toast, crème cup cakes, sweet rolls, cinnamon rolls, and many other toxic materials. That includes the boxed cereals full of sugar and grain starch with added sugar at finger tips on just about any restaurant counter or booth. It is hard to find I will tell ya. Not enough demand in America for a healthy breakfast. And look around just about any place with more than three people. There will be numerous obese and overweight people who should not have to have the futures they most likely will. Futures filled with diabetes, cardiovascular disease, and neurological disorders, Alzheimer's, tremors, Parkinson's and a host of still poorly defined inflammatory miseries.

Tanzer, however, could find the kind of place that was not a total toxic waste dump. Maybe some decent fruits, eggs, and green tea or kombucha for a beverage. I think finding the right kind of food is one thing that makes her so adorable, so prim, and so intelligent. She feeds her brain and her body the kind of fuel it needs to make strong bones, strong nerves, pliable veins, and does not overwork her vital parts like her pancreas, liver, thyroid, stomach, jejunum, and other workshops in her utterly lovely body.

We had eggs, fruit, berries, and some Canadian bacon the cook swore was natural organic, and without nitrites or other preservatives. Maybe it was, I did not have a chemical laboratory in my pocket to do an analysis, and independent inspectors of food are very rare in our profit driven culture. It is not likely any food an individual eats today has been checked by anyone who does not have a financial interest in cramming industrial waste products into our food supply so long as it is profitable to do so and does not cause immediate lethal effects that might alert the few functional agencies we have to investigate. Bad for business to over do on the toxic stuff to the point it can be traced to a particular brand. We left a nice tip for the trouble our waitress had to get the kind of food that passed El Tanzer's vigorous and intense inspection. A lot of jerks don't give a good waiter or waitress a good tip. Those are usually dumb arrogant sorts who don't know bad food when they see it. They just want the waitress to get it on the table as fast as possible so they can gorge on the waste and get on with their hectic lives. No time to savor good food with a friend, spouse, child, or man of knowledge.

So we left in good spirits, stopped at a modern gas station, filled the tank, checked the oil level, found it was low, bought a quart of oil. I did not really know what kind was right for my poor old abused iron horse. I washed the windshield that did not have very many bugs splatters on it, at least not the way it was in the good old days, checked the tire pressure, and down the road we went. I was brewing an idea in my mind. I would have to drive a while and see what developed. I have to do that from time to time. Just not force anything. Just see what develops.

Tanzer turned on this ancient radio that still worked. As we drove along I-90 we were treated to a talk show by none other than Lamar Lushmondle. I had on more than one occasion over the past fifteen years attempted to listen to an entire hour of Lamar Lushmondle ranting angrily about how completely off track my native land had gotten. Everything done by our national government was contrary to the way a free peoples ought to live. Every social program developed since the great depression was instituted by none other than Satan or at least one of Satan's lieutenants. A few of them had names according to Lamar; most were just referred to as "liberals."

Lamar cited the eternal truth revealed to him by Ayn Rand that every man is in fact an island, entitled to all the benefits of his own labor, his own creativity, and had no obligation to participate in any consortiums of his fellow citizens even unto helping to pay for roads. This Randian single omniscient island might use for any purpose even marketing of his single handed production, the labor and capital of someone else without giving a thought to his single handed good fortune by his own hand. The fiction novels from the pen of Ayn Rand had become reality to our airwave proselytizer Lamar. After five minutes it was clear that Lamar believed firmly in his occluded mind that there was such a thing as a free lunch.

Lamar also believed our national power was of such monumental strength that if any other nation on earth crossed us up, or would not sell us something we desired, from rum and bananas to slaves, to iron ingots, all that was necessary was for the U.S. to reach out a big clobbering paw and crush the fools in a single swat. Mr. Lushmondle was, however, completely opposed to either paying any soldiers or airmen that might be involved in the big swat by taxation, or borrowing by the government. He did not exactly enlighten the listening audience as to where such payments might come from except perhaps a more or less behind the scenes transfer of the means from poorer members of our culture. First no expenditures of public funds would occur to feed any destitute children. They, after all, could fend for themselves from garbage cans or gleaning fields of corporate farms who might, after extracting every penny they could, open the fields for a few days before snow falls so long as the gleaners might repair some fences or pick up rocks.

Lamar next commenced a lecture on why liberal women were all whores. I found this rant a bit offensive and looked over at Tanzer. She was, it turned out, very willing to allow me to terminate the raucous clubbing of common sense, bashing of ordinary decency, and the spewing forth of vitriol against the pursuers of things like finding the facts of whether the climate might be changing, species were becoming extinct, and most other scientific investigations. Investigations into healthful foods, prevention of cancer, or oversee food and drug safety were clearly not in the purview of public funding, according to Lamar.

So once again, hearing the opinion of Mr. Lushmondle put forth as the most important means of gaining the truth as declared by the Sophists of ancient Greece came to an end at approximately 22 minutes. This was one of the longest periods my ears were buffeted with what I had concluded were the miserable ravings of a man with severe chronic depression.

"I believe that some twenty five percent of the American population suffers from some mental condition or disorder that takes the joy and even the very functionality of living from them. I believe we were just listening to one so afflicted. Strangely, under the principle of birds of a feather flock together, there are large numbers of depressed people out there who find this stuff a confirmation of there own depressed view of life."

"Strange that so many advertisers support the stuff." Tanzer said.

"Money and profit rules the game. The advertisers don't care so long as the poor saps who waist their time with this angry depressed swill, go out and buy, buy, and buy. Of course they have a wide audience as in my view the stupiding of America is descending across our land like a great migration of dumb-birds had been given full certification to spew ignorance as a cure for depression."

We crossed over the Bozeman Pass just as a Burlington Northern Santa Fe coal carrier came roaring up the east approach. It was a big one with four headers of CW 44 diesel electric motive power on the front. Hoppers full of black stored solar energy recovered from ancient times where it had lain for millions of years in the Powder River Basin Coal fields.

"I remember what I learned from Edward Abbey in his book *The Journey Home*. Santa Fe means "Holy Faith." The Holy Faith Railroad had once been the master of transportation in the American Southwest arching up into the Great Plains where it was the Atchison Topeka, and Santa Fe Railroad. There engines proudly sported what was called the 'war bonnet' Silver engines with red noses. Once that Holy Faith railroad was free. Now it was interbred with the Northern Pacific, the Great Northern and the Chicago Burlington and Quincy. Now it belonged to one man in his Berkshire Hathaway mutual fund."

"You like railroads don't you?" Tanzer asked. "I noticed how you knelt down and felt the tracks back there in front of the bar where Ernst Hemingway drank."

"I do. They are awesome achievements of the human mind. Once they served the people. But not much any more. Hardly a passenger train left to any small towns. Just freight and only on lines that make the right amount of profit."

There were two pushers on the tail of the coal train. Big diesels burning oil to make the electric motors run that were moving the fossil Paleocene plant corpses to the furnaces and generators of China.

"Not many people would know those hoppers are full of Paleocene plant corpses turned to stone."

"I suppose." Tanzer said. "Only a nut like you would think of that."

"I might still be a little crazy or nutty as you call it. I am not sure when a person is, say, a little eccentric but nowhere near crazy. Or maybe a little nutty but quite sane, just different. I just am not sure where those boundaries are sometimes. For example take Galileo. He was quite sane in most modern minds but he was quite not sane in 1609 when he more or less proved that the earth was not the center of motion in the universe. To the majority in charge of mind clarification at the time this was heresy and thus Galileo was shown the instruments of torture, forced to recant the truths he had reported, and kept under house arrest until his death. Now just who was crazy? The principle bishops and the Holy Office of the Inquisition or the simple scientist who reported a few simple facts that conflicted with a long standing mental construct that his earthly cohabitants viewed as absolute truth based on ancient documents.

"Crazy is not so easy to ascribe to anyone seeking reality until there is a conflict with those who benefit from promulgation of an untrue myth. It is just something most do not have the courage to report upon and stand up to. It is dangerous to mess with the underpinnings of established rules. That the rules are based on falsehoods is not relevant to those wielding them for their own purposes."

At Livingston I had a sudden coruscation. I was going to completely circumbabulate the great caldera to the south. But when the time for a decision came I was inexorably drawn to follow the Yellowstone River. I would penetrate the great beast right into its heart.

"You will still have the option of a complete circumnabulation around the Big Tetons."

"Its Grand Tetons, Tanzerton. Grand Tetons."

"No matter. I will still come with you. I don't really have any pressing items on my agenda right now. Besides you still have not owned up to the real reason for this circumnabulation. So up the Yellowstone is fine."

Most of the time in places like the Paradise Valley, in fact, quite often in most places of the Rocky Mountain West, it is clear. Sometimes in the fall, winter, or spring, river valleys will develop some fog but not the kind the Pacific Ocean can create in a heartbeat. The dense blinding fog of the mighty oceans. But by the time we got within striking distance of the Roosevelt Arch, the river decided to fog up the place like it was competing with the Pacific Ocean in a foggy mood. It got so thick I could no longer drive on U.S. 89. Very unusual.

"We have to pull up till this fog moves out."

"It is cold out. Kind of clammy too."

We managed to find a camp site. Pure luck I could no longer see and there was a campsite. I wandered about and found some firewood from previous campers. It was sort of wet. I managed to split it with a Pulaski. I always have a Pulaski bolted to the bed of old Ben. Ben is the name I call my pickup in private moments, such as this. I usually don't tell any one its name but I think it will be ok this once.

"Ben, your truck is named Ben?" Tanzer seemed amazed.

"Yes, Ben is a guy truck. Some trucks are female trucks and some are guy trucks. I knew Ben was a guy the first time I drove him. You can tell if you know about it in the first place. Some people don't and think you are crazy if you ask them if their truck is a guy or a gal. Others, usually the smart creative types, already know this stuff."

Hot stew was simmering on the fire I eventually got going. Had to do a bunch of splitting to get some dry kindling but the Pulaski did the job.

"You used that on a fire last year. It was a lightening strike as I recall."

"And just how do you know that, Tanzer, the omniscient?"

"You know how."

We ate the stew and it started to darken. Would have to wait until the sunrise might clear this dense fog. I felt myself become more and more enshrouded in it.

I felt her hands gently massaging my neck. Then my very sore shoulder, the one that always flares up in dense cold fogs. I felt my mind go into a private lair, a place even I cannot adequately describe.

The church was quite ornately decorated. I was a few minutes late as I recall. It was, to tell you the truth, kind of a blur. I spent some time trying to figure out how to put on a tuxedo. I should have gotten direction at the tuxedo rental shop. Finally I got it on and somewhat adjusted. My best man was invaluable. He and I served in a war. It is not at all uncommon for people who serve in wars to become very deep friends. Especially if one or the other is wounded. Times like these when one gets married are bitter sweet. Each knows the one getting married will have a new deep relationship. Each worries a little he will lose a piece of his friend, his buddy who he went into hell with and came back. Still my best man had already married his sweetheart and as far as I was concerned was still not much changed. His wife was fine with giving him to me when we needed to be friends for a time. Last night for instance she said I could have him all to myself if I wanted. We both thought so much of his wife we wanted her to come and have dinner with us and just talk over whether I was making a really dumb mistake getting married. I was careful of course even with her there not to take anything from him that he should rightly give to her. She was remarkably unselfish though. I have high opinion of females who are not selfish with their husbands when it comes time to share them with old friends. It is not the most common trait in human females in my opinion.

So the next day came and we were standing at the front of this church in the apse or something like that. There were a lot more people than I thought would be there. Everyone was dressed to the nines as is usually required at big formal weddings. I was not entirely sure this was the right venue for me but it is what her family wanted. Her parents especially thought this was the only way the only place such things could be properly solemnized. I decided if her father needed to give her away it was not something I should stand in the way of. I actually believe it is best if a father thinks so much of his daughter that he cannot give her away, except in a ceremony such as this, where the poor lovesick man his daughter has decided belongs to her for the rest of eternity, is given with great sacred vows of love, fidelity, and so on, that he have the privilege of doing so.

Well anyway my friend, now my best man, and I are staring at this relatively large crowd that has migrated into rows of wooden pews, and now suddenly the organist is playing the Canon in D by Johann Pacabel when appears in the nave, or whatever they call it, is my gorgeous virgin, on the arm of her tuxedoed and very solemn father. I think she was on his left arm as I remember. Then the organist finishes the Canon at just the right moment, and a second or two of silence follows while everyone stands and turns to the rear. This is a completely idiotic thing to do as only the few on the aisle can see what everyone came to see. That of course is the beautiful bride in her white virgin dress. Does she look radiant, happy or is there a scintilla of doubt. The women, especially the married ones, and of course the young not yet engaged, and the uncertain ones, are most intent on this deep inspection. By uncertain I mean they have not yet decided if they ever want to be bound to a male. There are probably a lot more now who don't as the idea that a woman must be married to be a full member of society has crumbled into drastic little pieces and been swept under the national rug.

I think most of the men are more into whether the dress makes the bride look like she was in good physical condition and is suitable, well bred, and of unquestionable attractiveness that she is ready for a good screw. The more experienced men know, of course, that the wedding night is not the optimal time for such an introduction into the feminine mystery and pleasures as she is usually too exhausted from all the preparations, and fussiness involved in formal weddings. They know it is best if the man she has chosen for all time just helps her unzip her dress, perhaps have a private, very quiet glass of champagne, snuggle a little, and then get a good night sleep. There is plenty of time for her to unleash the procreative power of the universe and the male will be better able to take care of her delicious lust with his own and everything will be excellent if it is not forced by some stupid tradition that the wedding night is reserved for the defloration of virgins.

I worried about many things when the organist unleashed the wedding march and the father slowly brought the beautiful bride down the aisle for her inspection. She seemed however not to notice. She was looking straight at me the whole time. This fact gave me some solace that she cared more about me than any social status or satisfaction for the audience.

From that point on it was largely on auto pilot. Her father put her hand in mine and a robed fellow said "Who gives this woman to be married?" Her father said, "Her mother and I do." Then it was up before the altar, words were said, and rings put on. I suppose anyone who wants to know everything that was said, promised, ordained, and solemnized can look up in a standard wedding protocol for their particular religion and we can move forward. I do remember kissing my lady on her red lipsticked lips and taking a long look into her pretty sparkling eyes, the doorway to a woman's heart if you know about it. Her eyes were wide and I knew she was genuine and really meant it. What I did not know was there was a secret she had withheld from me. It had been withheld the entire three years I had gotten to know her. I was quite happy before I knew her but when I met her I stayed just as happy on most days but I was more happy when I was with her. So it had come down to this; a wedding and I believed we would live together in a cabin in the woods. I would cut firewood, and grow a garden full of sumptuous vegetables and berries, and fruits. I would hunt deer for winter meat and probably raise a hog. My bride would tend a small flock of chickens for eggs. She would, of course, make curtains for the cabin window that I had completely not thought of. I would go to work as a forest ranger that was my chosen thing. That was because I quite well loved trees and working in the woods. I was good at math, and science in general but I was frankly too stupid in advanced theoretical physics, rocket systems and molecular biology. I had no interest in medicine as I knew I would likely just as well dump a substantial number of my patients over the side of the nearest large chasm due to their being, for the most part, too greedy, too self centered, or desiring to destroy the natural world about them for some monetary profit or frankly just plain boring as hell.

I was standing at the back vestibule and the members of the congregation were filing past us shaking hands and wishing us all the happiness in the world and long lives and all that when a tall fellow who I thought was an airline pilot came up and shook hands with me and said' "Welcome to the Navy."

I did not exactly understand this as I had not enlisted in the Navy. In fact I had once been in the Marines, fulfilled a term of four years, been in a hot war with my buddy who was also here with me, gotten a few medals including a distinguished service and a purple heart and been honorably discharged. I never felt like much had been accomplished by the particular war my nation's leaders had gotten us into but I felt an obligation to serve before I knew what the nincompoops running the country had gotten us into. They do that from time to time I have noticed. It does not usually cost them anything. They don't get hurt or killed. They often get paid well. Some think they are committing soldiers, sailors, marines into a sacred action ordained by their God to do away with evil and make the world into a place their God can be proud of. That is proud of the nincompoop who got us involved in his war to begin with. Now don't get me wrong. I have explained to you before that I hold a Navy to be the best way our nation can be free of foreign scumbag emperors, kings, and others who seek to impose their will upon us. If I had to do it over I would have just joined the Navy in the first place. Then I would have worked my way onto a ship that was too god awful big to wade in any swamps or jungles or deserts belonging to some one else. A good many of these pestilent ridden fiefdoms can not seem to get even the most basic elements of their people to learn how to get along and so I see no reason for us to step in and try and make them.

We certainly need a Navy second to none to keep megalomaniacs and pirates off our shores. It ought to keep the sea lanes open for trade. It needs bases on islands, and some foreign shores and these need marines to keep the piece and secure the perimeter. I have mixed feelings about using land forces. Rarely have they been able to impose our will on foreign populations. That requires the co-option of local power structures to accomplish. Like we did in WWII. Like we did not do in Iraq. So until we must as a last resort commit ground troops overseas we must have a military objective followed by co-option of local leaders to ever achieve an overseas result worth the blood and treasure it takes to do diplomacy by force of arms on the ground.

Anyway this is when I left the receiving line, pulled on the bird captains arm, the one who I had first thought was an airline pilot, and asked him what he meant.

I learned the wonderful wife who was going to come and live happily ever after with me in a cabin in the woods was actually in the Navy and ranked as a Lieutenant Commander. She was a helicopter Squadron Commander operating off of an aircraft carrier. She had graduated from the U.S. Naval Academy and was, according to the Captain, a very distinguished pilot. I returned to my bride and just asked her "Are you in the Navy?"

"Yes." She said while continuing to shake hands of well wishers.

I more or less lost my cool here. I left the spot and wandered down a passageway until I found a vacant room. I was, to tell you the truth, in a state of shock. I had no idea and she had never brought up anything about being a naval officer. I think it was the fact that she had kept this from me. I could not fathom why she would have kept this from me. But the raw facts were now on the table. I was in a state of shock.

Then I became rather irritated. My mind was not working well at all. I could not have just gotten married. Not based on this kind of deception. I remember the preacher coming in with my bride saying, "We have to sign this certificate."

"I cannot sign that. I did not form the ineffable bond of becoming husband and wife today."

"You did." The preacher said rather annoyed.

"Does your church have an annulment ordinance? The kind the Roman tribunals adjudicate every day?" I asked. "I want to save a lot of trouble here. Just declare an error in the ceremony, an error in the "marriage" that "legal thing" did occur today. Perhaps we can continue to develop a relationship based on knowing the real other that will lead to becoming husband and wife. Perhaps not and we shall both be free to go on with our lives

"No. We have no such ordinance. You were pronounced husband and wife. You are joined in holy matrimony."

"There is something the matter here. I made a commitment to wed a woman who I did not know was also wed to the U.S. Navy. I don't know if this is ok with me. It might be or it might not be. I need time to mull this over, to get my feelings right with this new item that has suddenly intruded into my life. I am not good with not knowing this about my bride to be. I might be good with it and decide to wed her knowing this fact or I might not. But I must be free to choose that unencumbered by the legality of marriage. And marriage is a legal relationship not the ineffable bond of husband and wife."

"You are married, it has been done. It can not be undone in the kingdom of God."

"Sounds like from what you are telling me the only way I can have a chance to be husband to this woman is for me to obtain a secular divorce and then see if I can live with that. I need time to think about whether or not I want to be wed to a military pilot."

My bride was crying.

"I am the same person. It matters not what I do."

138

There was a reception coming up. Very shortly coming up. We were supposed to have a photographer record the sacred day in our lives. I did not wish to participate further in the day that had so suddenly turned into a big deception to me. I do not remember much of the rest of it. I walked, or more less was dragged, under an arch of swords. The whole time I was thinking about Tolstoy's War and Peace. It was utterly unnatural in eighteenth century Imperial Russia that men would stay at home and the women go to war. It had been that way in my native land too. Then things began to change. It took a while, I will admit. But change they did. No longer did the United States hold it an abomination to send its women into armed conflicts as warriors. Not that this was anything new. The ancient Amazons had gone into war. During World War II The Russians had changed their minds and sent three regiments of female pilots against the Luftwaffe and the Wehrmacht. The Russian women had shown beyond question that women could fight and become fighter aces and daring bomber pilots. No it was not competence as warriors that disturbed me. It was the big change in our culture that I was not yet prepared to embrace on a personal level. I still held a myth that the men protected the women. The thing I realized was that I had not caught up with my culture in my own personal life. I had a cognitive dissonance on top of all my other troubles.

I could not eat the wedding dinner nor respond appropriately to the toasts. I was just not in my right mind. I told my bride that I would be leaving for a two week journey into the wilderness behind the Grand Tetons. I would be leaving that very night in fact. It started to pour outside. It does that sometimes in the Puget Sound area. I like the rain but this night it was oppressive. I needed to just be by myself, make my way to the bus station or to SeaTac anything that could get me near the Grand Tetons. The rain came beating down in enormous rivers, the rain came pouring out of the night sky, the rain splattered on my face, soaking my tuxedo, dousing my spirit into an utter blackness. I could not find a path with lights. I was surrounded by soaking wet blackness and my heart seemed to be dead.

"Are you ok? Eltanzer asked.

I felt her holding me close to her. We were really more or less tangled up together. I could not figure out where I was. It took a few minutes to realize I had been deep in a dream. I was not in a soaking downpour in Puget Sound. I had not just been involved in a wedding, then a soul wrenching discovery upon learning I did not know who my new bride was.

"I think so." I replied in a fog. "Where am I?"

"The Valley of Paradise. You were having a bad dream. But it is over now. I am with you."

I sat up. I saw we had left a kettle on the fire. A swig of coffee might be in order. I suppose some would never consider coffee at this hour of the day but I am one whose genes do not react to coffee with the jitters or insomnia.

"Here you go," Tanzer said, handing me a cup

"How did you know I needed this?"

"You know. You are slow to change with the times. You prefer pickling to the boiling rage of change. I think I know now why you are on this circular safari around the big tits. I think I got it."

"Oh poof! O fuddy duddying, my darling, Tanzeroo. You are a Fig Newton. You Are a…."

"Don't call me a peach, or I'll smack you."

She meant it. I could see so I held my tongue. It is not always easy to keep one's tongue in a snare but things most often turn out better for those who learn to do it. I just imagine a Fig Newton in my mouth and wrestle it against the roof and don't let it get even a little bit loose.

"I need to believe in something," I said to Eltanzer. "What I used to believe in I no longer believe and there is a hole that gnaws at my being."

"I know," Eltanzer whispered.

"You know, of course you know, you always know."

The fog finally lifted the next day. We drove south along the famous Yellowstone River flowing free until it gets to eastern Montana. This is the river that created the Grand Canyon of the Yellowstone and drops over one of the most photographed and painted ledges in the yellow volcanic rhyolites. The river is the very artist itself that created Artists Point the famous painting site for capture of the artist tumbling over the lower falls. The volcano placed the yellow colored grist the artist cut through to frame itself surging in green drapes with white froth giving it a perpetual living shimmer.

For a time the Absaroka Range stood magnificently in the east for our passing inspection. We continued through the small town of Gardner and passed through the Roosevelt Arch Northern gateway to Yellowstone National Park. It was not long and a white hill came into view.

"There is something about that white hill that intrigues me." I mentioned.

"I know."

"You always know. Every time I say something like 'that white hill intrigues me' you say 'I know'."

"I know."

"Well, I want to stay at that white hill and explore it."

"If that is what is now required then that is what must be." Tanzer said.

I thought it was very Fig Newton of Tanzer to come up with that, but I did not say a word about it.

We came into Mammoth Hot Springs, one of the most enchanted places I know of in North America. And North America has some really enchanted places I can tell you. But this place has a mysterious quality to it that is mixed with a picturesque sensation that is enhanced with an olfactory phantasmagoria and, if one keeps his mouth shut, can provide little musical notes from time to time as carbon dioxide from deep in the earth fizzles in hot water.

I got us a room at the old historic Mammoth Hot Springs Lodge. A bunch of elk were also in residence, but as near as I could determine, paid no rental fees.

It was not long and we were hoofing it to the nearest pile of multicolored rock heaps known as travertine deposits. These heaps of calcium carbonate have been deposited over the millennia by hot waters seeping through fissures in the volcanic rocks from the hotter springs to the south. To avoid boredom the waters build up ledges, mounds, terraces, and pillars of travertine here and there and then, like all good conduits of flowing liquids, get clogged up from their own minerals and molecules and have to shift direction and find a new place to gurgle forth to the surface. All the while steaming and fizzing as they lay down new layers of travertine. It is not with out help from bacteria, archea, and algae that these layers are laid on the artist's palette. One of the nearest springs we come to is named Artist's Palette because of the many colored glistening travertines painted with the pigments of organisms called thermophiles. Many of the springs here have temperatures of 73 degrees centigrade yet thermophiles live in the hot water. As the water flows and laps over ledges the species of the microbes change along lowered temperature gradients and many become a different color from brown, red, orange, and green.

"You like this don't you?" Tanzer announces. "You are really excited by this array of life. I can tell you are getting more and more ok in the mind. I can tell you are returning to being among the sane of the earth."

"Oh sure you can tell."

I realized there were getting to be times that the arrogance of my beautiful traveling companion sort of stuck under my saddle like a chinkapin burr. Chinkapin burrs can be a little bit annoying or greatly annoying depending upon whether they remain static or move around reaching more tender sensitive positions around the softer regions of ones hiney. Or is it highney?

I can never seem to remember how to spell it. She was right though. Just being in the presence of these, the modal forms of life on this planet today, yesterday and, as near as any of the best biologists and paleomicrobiologists can tell, from the beginning they were the first cellular forms of life on this planet. They have been at this kind of work for billions of years whether building stromatolites in the shallow bays of oceans or painting rocks in the cracks and fissures of enormous volcanoes such as the one we are now standing upon. I of course want to know all the species that are here. But they are still being classified and there are critters of affiliation we know not.

"I think if we ever come to know just how these little things came to be we shall have answered a primal question of man. Where did we come from and what are we?" I told Tanzer.

"Would you really want to know or would you prefer a creation story that might be more comforting than how these kinds of organisms came to create consortia that likely, over eons, assembled you and the elk over there?"

"I would rather know the truth, the flat out truth."

"Even if it meant you have a finite existence, even if you came from rock dwelling microbes that assembled in unconscious little heaps and learned to do the complex biochemistry it takes to run your body?"

"Especially if that is the truth. I suppose that is the way of this little tiny bunch of spiritual descendants, known today as scientists, from the likes of Galileo, Pasteur, Darwin, Wallace, Archilocus, Epicurus, and Einstein stood against ignorance and moved us a little closer to the truth. Some of us must know the reality before we can believe the mythology."

"Tonight I will take you to a special place here, one that not many know about, ok?" the annoying but most alluring one pronounced.

"I suppose I have no option like sleeping in a warm bed all night?" I replied.

"Of course you have that option but I know you won't select it." Eltanzer purred.

"Of course you know. Of course you know." I groused

It was on the order of 2 am when I was rousted out of the bed that took a long time to warm up in the first place, and we trudged along a road vacated of the usual horde of steel carriages, buses, ranger patrols, and trampling feet of the tourists who come for a few moments then leave with little understanding of what they have seen. One of my feet got sore as I had a lumpy sock on and did not have the sense to stop and refit. I was a little anxious, to tell you the truth, that this adventure was likely to involve an encounter with a grizzly bear, or a mad bull elk, or a pack of wolves, or even a giant *Anhaunguera* that had escaped the notice of modern biologists. It seemed possible that boneheads could come crashing out of the sulphur smelling heaps of travertine and decide we needed a good butting. These, by the way, are also known as Pachycephalosaurs of the Cretacious Period who developed very thick skulls and who enjoyed butting heads apparently to see who could breed with whom in the *Pachycepholasaurus* world. It may be the model upon which more modern humans have decided to operate government societies such as Congresses. That is just a speculation on my part but it seems more or less true.

Along we went. Plod, plod, tramp, tramp, one foot after another on the thick beds of travertine under the asphalt roadway. The one who I held in mysterious esteem keeping me company.

She broke the noise of our footsteps saying "I really want to make love with you tonight. I am really tired of your reluctance to make love to me. You know you want to make love yet you are bound by that promise you made so long ago. We must see what we can do about that."

"No matter what I say or do, no matter what I think about, you always know I want to make love to you. You always know I can not look into your deep brown eyes without falling apart inside. You just love to torture me with your allure. Don't you Tanzer, my darling."

"I do not torture you. I would never do such a thing to you. You know very good and well I don't. So just stop making up this hogwash."

"Hogwash, just hog wash." I grumbled.

"Turn on this trail, right over here. We are going to do something important. Something that has to be done."

We took the trail that the charge boss of this dark hour commanded. There were stars out. Very bright stars I must admit. Until one goes into a terrifying night with no way to stop it, one cannot understand the comfort, the wonder that starlight can bring to a place. In fact the starlight can even assuage the fear one feels when traipsing about a volcanic vent, a steaming volcanic vent at that, one that according to the warning signs could involve suddenly crashing through a thin travertine cover and falling into a pot of hot water, that, while not boiling, is still hot enough to do serious cooking of a human body. Then it appeared. A great whitish glowing heap.

"This is what I wanted you to behold." El Tanzer, the radiant one, purred.

I was rather suddenly overcome by a strange feeling. I felt as if I was in the presence of a supernatural power. I don't believe in supernatural powers as I believe we have previously established. So it could not be a supernatural power. Still there it was, a transcendent pathway I was on, one that I could not explain by the general rules of biology, nor could I perform an integral calculation that gave me any mathematical direction as to what was going on.

"You are struggling with this aren't you?" she asked.

"Struggling, I suppose so. If that is what you are going to call it. A struggle. What is real, what is not real? What is going on in my mind that might be looking at something real or am I creating something real that only exists in my mind?"

"Do not lie to me. You do love this great, snow white, creation. I know your heart so don't tell me otherwise."

I turned suddenly and took EL Tanzer in my arms and pulled her tight to my body. I took her wrists in my hands and slowly moved them behind her back. I wanted her in my embrace, in my power. I felt the shiver and the tension build. It was raw animal tension, a desire so intense there was nothing I could do to stop it. Maddening it was too. I do not just yield to the forces of nature. I stand pat on my principles, my beliefs and I keep my promises.

"We are in her temple." Tanzer whispered in my ear.

"Whose temple? Don't get me off on temples. You know I do not believe in temples."

"You are in one. This one is Minerva's temple. They call it Minerva's terrace and it used to run water all the time. Like when you first came here so many years ago. But now the spring has let the terrace dry for a while. That is the way. Change is always going on. Nothing stays the same for long. And here you can experience that change ordained by the goddess, The Roman goddess Minerva who the Greeks knew as Athena Parthenos, Athena the Virgin. Athena was the goddess of wisdom, and of civilization. She had changed her name under the Romans as the daughter of Jupiter. She sprang fully armed from the greatest god's head. I can see her standing with a great shield on the top ledge of the glowing white terrace."

I looked into the eyes of the goddess herself who I was holding in my arms who had totally rendered me incapable of defending myself against her mysterious but magnetic allure. I suddenly grasped the power that the ancients must have experienced in a situation like this. There was this feeling that more was going on, much more than just being here looking at stones. I experienced this aliveness that was more overbearing than I had experienced on any other days. But as I thought long and hard I came to realize that maybe I had experienced this kind of aliveness on many days.

"Now have I helped you understand the encounter with life better?" Tanzer asked.

"Are you real, Tanzer?"

"Of course I am real. Don't you understand what real is?"

"No. Yes. Maybe. You seem real enough but then you don't seem the same as ordinary real. Different maybe, but real all the same."

"I am real because I formed in your mind. We are not leaving until you love me with all your heart and soul one more time. Just once more you must love me as if I was a real woman of your dreams. Like you were madly aroused by my charms. You must without omission feel the same love you had for me when you sat by the bloodroot clump, the first conscious thing in your mind. It must be that intense joy of first becoming conscious and knowing you exist and are not alone. Then you must let me go. I desire that you let me go. I give you permission to love the sagebrush, and the alpine fir, The Grand Tetons, and the snow white terrace. You can remember me but you must no longer let love for me tear you asunder. I desire you no longer pine for me."

There was a kind of blur. I remember walking north for some time. We walked hand in hand in the starlit night, coming to the Liberty Cap, a long dead pile of weathered travertine. There were no people about, not at this hour. Some running water gurgled a little bit, not a lot but just a little bit. It was probably a message from the goddess that she was hard at work building some new temples for future generations of tourists to come and see and have little understanding of. Some might think God had created the whole thing in one swell pronouncement and that the things here never changed over what was here at the exact time of the tourists visit. A few would know this was a work of art in progress that came into being when the mysterious forces of the earth placed the hotspot of a huge volcano at this location for the time being. How long would the earth abide this place for hot springs and geysers? No one knows. For it has been some 640,000 years since the earth erupted here last and blew things like Mammoth Hot Springs into dust. Then, over the millennia, moved the minerals into Palette Springs, and the Orange Mound. Upon them grew the descendents of ancient beings, beings who we cannot see with our naked eye but who colored the snow-white carbonate with many hues. Here one can be with the ancient archea, cyanobacteria, algae, the eubacteria, and all the modal living things on this planet.

We returned to the room where the bed was utterly cold. I climbed in and began the task of warming it up. Tomorrow we would venture into the old caldera itself. I tried but I could not be sure what happened up there in the temple of the ancient goddess. It was like Tanzer drew some curtain over my eyes and would not let me know what had happened up there. I wondered if I had made love to her as she demanded of me. I thought I must have made love to her. How could I not have made love to her. I was in agony over this uncertainty. How could she do this to me?

Tanzer was sound asleep. I was going to ask her what had transpired. I was a trifle annoyed that she was sleeping when I needed desperately to know what really had happened. I reached over to shake her a little bit but as soon as I touched her shoulder something made me stop. I pulled back and rolled on my side.

We got up in the morning and had a superb breakfast at the Mammoth Lodge Inn. I was a little reluctant to leave the hot springs but we needed to finish this penetration into the enormous caldera. I needed to finish some important business. I had to become, I had to become.....

We spent some time hand in hand walking the boardwalks of the Norris Geyser Basin. Steam rose here and there from very hot springs. Streamers of green algae waved in the flowing waters as they cooled on the surface. One I recognized was *Cyanidium caldarum*. I had once been fascinated to peer into a microscope and see tiny cells of an algae that grew in my lake. The lake that was for so long my home. We wandered to the steaming hole that is the world's largest geyser. Steamboat Geyser. It is persnickety. It erupts when it feels like erupting but with no regular pattern. Today it just steamed. We continued to Echinus, the acidic geyser that is more reliable but takes a long time if you just missed it spouting by a few minutes. We were lucky. After an hour it put forth a great shower of fairly cold water for a geyser. It is one of the few you can sit in the spray and not get burned. A walk to the Green Dragon Spring followed. Everywhere the great show of an active volcano captured our imaginations. There was a place where the Fringed Gentian bloomed. We stopped to become engulfed in the captivating glory of the blue muses of the Rocky Mountains. Nowhere do they match the mysterious array of life as those who dare to live on the roof of a boiling volcano.

All too soon it was time to move on. We passed into the country of the Grand Canyon of the Yellowstone. Holding hands we took in the great green falls plunging in white foamy embroidery over the ledge of rhyolite, one of the two main rocks created directly by the volcano. The air danced with the rock to create a soft yellow patina that gave the region its name, The Great Yellowstone Ecosystem. I began to wake up. Once I was here many years ago. Holding hands with El Tanzer. Then just as now.

We left the deep chasm and meandered our way south through the Mud Volcano and the Sulphur Caldron solfataras. Here the scientists have discovered the Archea *Sulfolobus* an organism that converts hydrogen sulphide into sulphuric acid. As I watched the steaming caldron, I brought forth from memory of a long time ago watching the Mother of Vinegar hard at work on the crock of cider. A small unseen worker tirelessly converting the ethyl alchohol of hard cider into acetic acid. I did not know, when I first saw these brown muds so long ago, that an unseen organism could possibly be alive and at work in those stinking muds. Those muds suddenly reminded me of spilling the chocolate malt on the young snobby girl's dress so long ago. My god how those things stay with us.

We drove on through the Hayden Valley filled with elks, along the Yellowstone River to its source at Yellowstone Lake. Tanzer and I sat on a dock behind the yellow Lake Hotel and watched the sunset over the deep blue waters. The Lake Hotel had elegance to it. It was manmade but still it seemed not out of place as large lodging facilities now so often do. Our cities are strip malled not only with stores but also with lodges that seem designed more for the lodges to grab a quick buck than to serve as places where the human spirit can come alive. Here the spirit was at rest.

As the sun went down Tanzer said. "Have you been feeling the full love for me of your youth?"

"I have. You were my first love. I know what I must do. But it hurts. Will you tell me once more what it was like, like you were there with me?"

Tanzer said, "I remember the first time you knew me. I should more correctly say 'when you created me.' It was a wonder to behold, the emergence of the snowdrops through melting snows, Crocus and daffodils were next then tulips and azaleas. When the dogwoods were in bloom and the spring sky was dazzling azure. You lay there and watched the crossed petals in their springtime glory. All the kids were fond of noticing the brown notches on the tips and the anthers that resembled a crown of thorns. There was among you a legend that the dogwood was the tree that the Romans made the cross on which they crucified Rabbi Yeshua. Of course it was not long and you determined that was just a local story. It could not be correct because dogwood did not grow in ancient Palestine. You learned there are always local legends to make stories fit the familiar.

"There was the time when you were sixteen and you and I went on this long adventure. We walked on a mountain in the Valley and Ridge Geologic Province. We walked the Tuscarora Mountain and we had to stop and examine the ancient rocks of the once great Appalachian Range. That range so old it no longer rises thousands of feet above the sea as it did many millions of years ago. As you know it rose, probably starting in Cambrian times, the same time as the Flathead sandstones were laid down that now are exposed in a few places on the young up-thrust of the Grand Tetons and are the same sandstone we walked on at the Great Unconformity not so long ago. The basement rocks of the East and the West are much the same. When they were laid down there was no East and West of America. There was only a craton and it was in the southern hemisphere. It might help you to think of that from time to time. We loved the deep green of the forest. You could not help but desire to know every tree. You were not satisfied until you could walk up to the gray barked beech and know it as *Fagus grandifolia* or the great red oak as *Quercus rubra*. It took a while to get good at the lesser known such as the Atlantic white cedar *Thuja occidentalis*. Those you saw when we camped in the Adirondack range. The red spruce we figured out on old granite hills. Some, like the eastern white pine and the hemlock came fairly easily. In the Highlands Province we

150

learned the bitternut hickory. The mocker nut was harder unless you could find the nuts. There were the magnificent grey birches *Betula populifolia* that adorned so much of the landscape that made the superb firewood for the Christmas fire and black walnuts that made the tasty meat in hard black shells. Of course you fell in love with my sugar maples *Acer saccharum* that you ran in the early spring to make the deep golden amber maple syrup. You worked so hard to learn every tree.

"On soils, made from Jurrasic age sediments, you grew the most delicious tomatoes, sweet corn, watermelons, peaches, currents, and peas. The leaves of autumn you piled into great heaps that after two years rotted to make a natural fertilizer. Snow apples, Macintosh, and Jonathans grew the sweetest fruits. The summer brought forth the Montmorency Cherries renowned for pies and jelly. The summer evenings brought forth the lover flashes of the fire flies while katydids sang in the tree tops. Screech owls spoke of mysterious things during hot sweltering summer nights.

"There were hurricanes that took down some of the great trees and took out the power lines. In the winter when Orion and his dogs filled the night sky with brilliant stars there were ice storms that laid the birch trees low to the ground. When the power lines came down from the heavy burdens of ice and broken trees then birch logs in the fireplace heated the house. Snowmen emerged in front yards and the third Wachung Hill became a sledding run. I was with you and the other kids for the toboggan runs on the old dairy meadow. I was with you when you fed the tufted titmouse and the white throated sparrow sunflower seeds and the chickadees with peanut butter globs. I was with you when the spring winds made for flying kites in the fields of bluestem grass that still adorned the earth."

We left the shore of the great Yellowstone Lake. I got us a room at the Lake Hotel. We went to the elegant dining room, a place with a lot of history. Tanzer was utterly magnificent in a white trimmed maroon evening gown. At dinner she was the biggest attraction, I could tell. These old white haired men would keep sneaking glances at her. Their wives often noticed and of course gave them a frown. I knew my Tanzer was beautiful. I made her that way from the beginning.

We had trout amandine for dinner. It was all very elegant in the dim lights of the historic hotel.

"You had trout amandine here the first time we came here." Tanzer said.

"I know. I caught it myself and brought it here and the chefs cooked it. That seems so long ago now."

"It was just an instant you know. Just an instant."

We finished dinner and wandered a little outside. The sky was unbelievably clear. No city lights to obscure the heavens. Rising in the eastern sky was the virgin with her brilliant star, Spica, shining on Lake Yellowstone. I was holding the virgin's hand as I felt the eternity of deep time and the glory of the short time of a human life. I felt a strange understanding in the quiet night.

"If you get lonesome for me just look up," Eltanzer whispered. "For he who learns the stars is always able to visit home."

Here on top of a great steaming volcano I felt some kind of reality and it was both terrifying and serene at the same time. Nothing lasts forever. There will come a time when this enormous volcano erupts and will likely do so much destruction that the continued existence of the United States will be in jeopardy. It may even be enough to severely cool the earth so that land is unable to grow crops to feed the billions of people that now inhabit the earth. The oceans have become already so depleted of many fish that even the mighty seas will not sustain us. Massive chaos and violence of the crazed starving and sick survivors will mark the earth. One of these volcanoes, of which there are now at least a half dozen known, are the most likely limits to the domination of man on the Earth. The volcano is a short interval catastrophic disrupter of the ecosystem. Sometimes it is just a local disrupter but at other times it is global. The small ups and downs of global climate swings are likely accounted for by volcanic events on a short term scale. Then there are intermediate level disrupters. And on the scale of deep time are the major events that mark the geologic periods we recognize in the fossil record. Events like gamma ray bursts from dying stars thousands of light years away, and impactors of rock or ice, such as the Cretaceous impactor that finished off the 160 million year reign of the great dinosaurs. Tremendously successful for those eons, the great lizards could not stand the earth wide catastrophe of that relatively small in size but high energy space missile that crossed orbits with the third planet 65 million years ago. There are huge atmospheric gas catastrophes such as the one billions of years ago that unleashed oxygen on an anaerobic world and events of hydrogen sulphide and methane releases that are murderous on living ecosystems.

Knowing the raw facts that the universe just does not care about the survival of species is unsettling until one just accepts the way things really are. I decided right then that acceptance of being a biological species that will likely join the millions of other extinct species at some unknown destiny in this great mystery, the cosmos, and then living every moment with as much joy as possible. Acceptance of these realities is the mark of a sane man.

We slept very soundly that night. In the morning Tanzer was gone. I was not greatly surprised about this. I expected it would happen. In fact she had foretold and insisted it would happen. I knew I would have to let her go. Who was my traveling companion since she emerged from the Snake River? She was a composite phantom I created and carried with me. I reified my love for the eastern forests, lakes, hills, and meadows into a woman. The mountains and trees, the granite outcrops, and the ancient limestone beds. The colonial houses and gardens, the place I first knew as home. Her name derived from a nebulous thing my mind created. **E**astern **L**and **T**rees and **N**ortheast **Z**est **E**nchanted **R**ealm. From the first letters of each word, Eltanzer emerged. Some strange working, of my all to human mind, did this. It was to help me with the pain of a loss of my love for the verdant east while being now a long time citizen of the arid west. I knew until I felt the pain of loss, and came to terms with it I would not be at peace. Starlight let me put Eltanzer to rest in a quiet grave. Eltanzer would like a real person, never be entirely lost. She would live in memory and that is a part of my reality.

I got out of bed and saw there was an envelope on the small bed side table. On its face was written: "To be sane and at peace a man needs a mythos that is in accord with reality."

A short note was written on a postcard next to an envelope.

"Take this envelope to the Snake River near Moose, Wyoming and there unseal it. Lift up your eyes unto the mountains and breathe in their grandeur. Open the envelope and read what is written.

Ps: Thank you for coming to my funeral and listening to my little talk. I think you knew all along it was me we were placing in the ground. I know it must have been hard for you but you have to live the destiny you chose. I will always be in your heart; be a part of you but you must not pine for me any longer."

I allowed myself to shed a last tear, while I placed Eltanzer in a shining memory in my mind. And I knew I must obey her last command and pine no more.

I drove to West Thumb, a funny side bay on Yellowstone Lake. There is a thermal area here and I wandered about the hot springs and paint pots that continued to steam and plop mud and stink. Then I drove south to the front of the Grand Tetons. I followed her directions and found a secluded spot along the quietly flowing river.

I opened the envelope and removed a nice crisp document. It had writing on it in what I recognized as my familiar hand.

The Tenets of a Naturalist

I emerged from the eons into a consortium of prokaryotic and eukaryotic cells that mysteriously became conscious. I don't know what my consciousness is, it is a great mystery. I draw upon my senses to observe the natural world. I feed upon the bread of knowledge baked over centuries by seekers of truth. A natural history emerges from events in past eons, from the structures of matter, and the remains of the grand mystery, life. One's mind examines the cosmos for its history in quasars, galaxies, stars and the near at hand rocks of our planet. I learn the stars for they go with me. No matter where I roam I find home among the stars.

Hypothesis testing exposes false conceptions and discards them while moving closer to truth by eliminating the fog covering truth with shrouds of ignorance. Nothing is proven. It only moves us closer to truth. Perhaps one day we shall improve its imperfections.

I find joy while enquiring into the mythos of the human mind. Stories that come from the distant fountains of former human thought form the grist of my inquiry. The stories of most fascination are those portraying the primordial worldview of our ancestors. These are the beings that first possessed and cultured the same kind of brain as we their progeny, the only known minds powerful enough to ask of the universe "why?" The answers tell and re-tell stories that give meaning to each generation. As fossils link us to primordial life, the myths link us to ancient quests and ancient answers.

Out of an ever changing and evolving palette of knowledge and myth from ancient and extant cultures I form my own novel story. I must know my own story, who the character in the drama is that I have been cast to play. My act lasts as a brief candlelight in time for I have rejected the purveyors of consciousness or eternal life after death. I have accepted the joy of life knowing it is ephemeral. It is death that is eternal peace in an insensate void. Knowing who I am, I can form relationships that light my little place with meaning. I can see that

I am not one unitary thing but a living community of bacterial and eukaryotic dynamos that compose and play a mysterious symphony. I can join in a concert with my brothers and sisters and snuff out loneliness for the vastness of space and time can easily leave me very alone. For special others the light of love shines in my heart and beyond.

All too soon, as it was written by an ancient but unknown sage, and at an hour and place I know not, my flame will go out, and my home will know me no more. Then I shall be subsumed into the mystery of eternal peace and be conscious no more.

When I finished reading the words I looked up. Towering above me, in snow-clad glory, reined the Grand Teton Range, the youngest mountains in America. Young as the mountains are, they are made of the ancient metamorphosed rocks laid down in a Proterozoic sea billions of years ago. The old battered and twisted rocks exposed here have become something new. That seemed a good way for me to think of myself. I was at ease for I had come to terms with the love of my youth, the gentle mist shrouded east, and the love of my old age, the arid expanse of the west. Charlorain I called her. **C**harming **A**rid **L**ands **O**f **R**aging **I**nterest. I could not call home both the east with her magnificent hardwood forests of oak and hickory, and the West with the expanses of big sagebrush and conifer skirted mountains. I had to make a choice of which would be home. I had chosen the West but I learned, having done so, I needed to let go of the East. Still it was the stars that reigned over both east and west. Eltanzer said look up and you will again be with me for they are the same. I knew I must let the inner love storm subside and that we must all make hard choices in life and live by them. More importantly, I had exercised my consciousness and made my own ephemeral lifetime meaningful to me. I had become satisfied with my life decision and was at peace before the Grand Tetons.

Thank you, Eltanzer, the cradle of my life. And maybe you cleared my mind and taught me I should stop resisting the light of love that shines in the eyes of the real woman who lives down in the valley. You know the one I mean and the whole story.

Allagash Rivers

About the Author

Robert L. Wooley spent his childhood in eastern forests where he learned woodsmanship. After he became a botanist and forester, he migrated to the west where he worked as a forest ecologist and entomologist, botanist, and forester in several locations including Yellowstone. He now resides in Dillon, Montana.